Pokémon BLACK VERSION

HANDBOOK

STATS AND FACTS ON OVER 150 BRAND-NEW POKÉMON!

Pokémon WHITE VERSION

ISBN 978-0-545-31652-1

Published by Scholastic Inc.
SCHOLASTIC and associated logos are trademarks and/or registered trademarks of Scholastic Inc.

12 11 10 9 8 7 6 5 4 3   11 12 13 14 15/0

Designed by Henry Ng and Two Red Shoes Design
Printed in the U.S.A.   40
First printing, August 2011

P9-DCC-088

Scholastic Inc.

| New York | Toronto | London | Auckland |
| Sydney | Mexico City | New Delhi | Hong Kong |

MEET THE POKÉMON OF UNOVA!

Welcome to the Unova region! Unova is the setting for the newest Pokémon video games, *Pokémon Black Version* and *Pokémon White Version*. Here people live in harmony with many rare and unusual Pokémon.

The Pokémon you may have encountered in Kanto, Johto, Hoenn, and Sinnoh are rarely seen in Unova. This region is made up of many acres of wilderness, but it's also home to Castelia City, with its busy streets and towering skyscrapers.

New Trainers in Unova receive their first Pokémon from Professor Juniper. We've got all the info you'll need when choosing between three new Pokémon: Snivy, Tepig, and Oshawott.

This book contains what you need to know about over 150 of Unova's brand-new Pokémon species. Each of these new Pokémon has its own Ability and unique powers, and we've got the inside scoop on all of them.

We've listed all the Pokémon alphabetically, so it will be easy to find the one you're looking for. Each page is packed with useful facts about that Pokémon.

HOW TO USE THIS BOOK

Here are the basics you'll discover about each Pokémon...

NAME

CATEGORY OF POKÉMON

HOW TO SAY IT
Some of those Pokémon names are pretty tough to pronounce! So we're breaking it down syllable by syllable.

UNOVA POKÉDEX NUMBER
Every Pokémon in Unova has its own unique number in the Unova Regional Pokédex.

POSSIBLE MOVES
Each Pokémon has a special set of moves it can use in battle. We'll show you some of the moves that a Pokémon can learn as it levels up.

TYPE
Every Pokémon is associated with one or more types. (More on this on the next page!) A Pokémon can also be a combination of two different types—this is called a dual-type Pokémon.

ABILITY
Each Pokémon has an Ability that can help it in battle. A Pokémon's Ability usually relates back to its type in one way or another. Some Pokémon have one of two possible Abilities.

HEIGHT & WEIGHT

DESCRIPTION
Every good Trainer wants to learn as much as he or she can about new Pokémon. This book includes all the Pokédex info about each Pokémon.

EVOLUTION
If your Pokémon has an evolved form or a pre-evolved form, we'll show you its place in the chain and how it evolves.

Want to understand more about Pokémon types?
Keep reading!

POKÉMON TYPES

Every Pokémon has a type — like Grass, Water, or Fire. Type tells you a lot about a Pokémon, including what moves it's likely to use in battle and where it likes to live. For example, Fire-type Pokémon usually enjoy hot, dry places like volcanoes. They may use attacks such as Flamethrower or Fire Spin. Grass Pokémon prefer to get tons of sunlight. They use attacks like Vine Whip and Razor Leaf.

Type also helps you figure out which kind of Pokémon will do well in a battle against another type. Water dampens Fire, and Fire scorches Grass. Flying-types have an advantage over Ground-types. But Ground-types take the charge out of Electric-types.

There are seventeen different Pokémon types:

Fire

Grass

Water

Normal

Electric

Bug

Ghost

Flying

Fighting

Psychic

Steel

Rock

Ground

Ice

Poison

Dark

Dragon

Okay, Trainers, are you ready to begin your journey through Unova? Then turn the page and let's get started!

ACCELGOR
SHELL OUT POKÉMON

HOW TO SAY IT: ak-SELL-gohr
POKÉDEX NUMBER: 123
TYPE: Bug
ABILITY: Hydration/Sticky Hold
HEIGHT: 2' 07"
WEIGHT: 55.8 lbs.
POSSIBLE MOVES: Leech Life, Acid Spray, Double Team, Quick Attack, Struggle Bug, Mega Drain, Swift, Me First, Agility, Giga Drain, U-turn, Bug Buzz, Recover, Power Swap, Final Gambit

POKÉMON BLACK VERSION:
When its body dries out, it weakens. So, to prevent dehydration, it wraps itself in many layers of thin membrane.

POKÉMON WHITE VERSION:
Having removed its heavy shell, it becomes very light and can fight with ninja-like movements.

Link Trade Karrablast and Shelmet

Shelmet → Accelgor
EVOLUTIONS

ALOMOMOLA
CARING POKÉMON

HOW TO SAY IT: uh-LOH-muh-MOH-luh

POKÉDEX NUMBER: 100

TYPE: Water

ABILITY: Healer/Hydration

HEIGHT: 3' 11"

WEIGHT: 69.7 lbs.

POSSIBLE MOVES: Pound, Water Sport, Aqua Ring, Aqua Jet, DoubleSlap, Heal Pulse, Protect, Water Pulse, Wake-Up Slap, Soak, Wish, Brine, Safeguard, Helping Hand, Wide Guard, Healing Wish, Hydro Pump

POKÉMON BLACK VERSION: The special membrane enveloping Alomomola has the ability to heal wounds.

POKÉMON WHITE VERSION: Floating in the open sea is how they live. When they find a wounded Pokémon, they embrace it and bring it to shore.

DOES NOT EVOLVE

AMOONGUSS
MUSHROOM POKÉMON

HOW TO SAY IT: uh-MOON-gus
POKÉDEX NUMBER: 097
TYPE: Grass-Poison
ABILITY: Effect Spore
HEIGHT: 2' 00"
WEIGHT: 23.1 lbs.
POSSIBLE MOVES:
Absorb, Growth, Astonish, Bide, Mega Drain, Ingrain, Faint Attack, Sweet Scent, Giga Drain, Toxic, Synthesis, Clear Smog, SolarBeam, Rage Powder, Spore

POKÉMON BLACK VERSION: It lures prey close by dancing and waving its arm caps, which resemble Poké Balls, in a swaying motion.

POKÉMON WHITE VERSION: They show off their Poké Ball caps to lure prey, but very few Pokémon are fooled by this.

Foongus → Level 39 → Amoonguss

EVOLUTIONS

ARCHEN
FIRST BIRD POKÉMON

HOW TO SAY IT: AR-ken
POKÉDEX NUMBER: 072
TYPE: Rock-Flying
ABILITY: Defeatist
HEIGHT: 1' 08"
WEIGHT: 20.9 lbs.

POSSIBLE MOVES: Quick Attack, Leer, Wing Attack, Rock Throw, Double Team, Scary Face, Pluck, AncientPower, Agility, Quick Guard, Acrobatics, DragonBreath, Crunch, Endeavor, U-turn, Rock Slide, Dragon Claw, Thrash

POKÉMON BLACK VERSION: Said to be an ancestor of bird Pokémon, they were unable to fly and moved about by hopping from one branch to another.

POKÉMON WHITE VERSION: Revived from a fossil, this Pokémon is thought to be the ancestor of all bird Pokémon.

Archen

Level 37

Archeops

EVOLUTIONS

ARCHEOPS
FIRST BIRD POKÉMON

HOW TO SAY IT: AR-kee-ops
POKÉDEX NUMBER: 073
TYPE: Rock-Flying
ABILITY: Defeatist
HEIGHT: 4' 07"
WEIGHT: 70.5 lbs.

POSSIBLE MOVES: Quick Attack, Leer, Wing Attack, Rock Throw, Double Team, Scary Face, Pluck, AncientPower, Agility, Quick Guard, Acrobatics, DragonBreath, Crunch, Endeavor, U-turn, Rock Slide, Dragon Claw, Thrash

POKÉMON BLACK VERSION: They are intelligent and will cooperate to catch prey. From the ground, they use a running start to take flight.

POKÉMON WHITE VERSION: It runs better than it flies. It catches prey by running at speeds comparable to those of an automobile.

Archen

Level 37

Archeops

EVOLUTIONS

AUDINO
HEARING POKÉMON

HOW TO SAY IT: AW-dih-noh

POKÉDEX NUMBER: 037

TYPE: Normal

ABILITY: Healer/Regenerator

HEIGHT: 3' 07"

WEIGHT: 68.3 lbs.

POSSIBLE MOVES: Pound, Growl, Helping Hand, Refresh, DoubleSlap, Attract, Secret Power, Entrainment, Take Down, Heal Pulse, After You, Simple Beam, Double-Edge, Last Resort

POKÉMON BLACK VERSION:
It touches others with the feelers on its ears, using the sound of their heartbeats to tell how they are feeling.

POKÉMON WHITE VERSION:
Its auditory sense is astounding. It has a radarlike ability to understand its surroundings through slight sounds.

DOES NOT EVOLVE

AXEW
TUSK POKÉMON

HOW TO SAY IT: AKS-yoo
POKÉDEX NUMBER: 116
TYPE: Dragon
ABILITY: Rivalry/Mold Breaker
HEIGHT: 2' 00"
WEIGHT: 39.7 lbs.

POSSIBLE MOVES: Scratch, Leer, Assurance, Dragon Rage, Dual Chop, Scary Face, Slash, False Swipe, Dragon Claw, Dragon Dance, Taunt, Dragon Pulse, Swords Dance, Guillotine, Outrage, Giga Impact

POKÉMON BLACK VERSION: They use their tusks to crush the berries they eat. Repeated regrowth makes their tusks strong and sharp.

POKÉMON WHITE VERSION: They mark their territory by leaving gashes in trees with their tusks. If a tusk breaks, a new one grows in quickly.

Axew   ▶ Level 38   Fraxure   ▶ Level 48   Haxorus

EVOLUTIONS

BASCULIN
HOSTILE POKÉMON

Red-Striped Form

HOW TO SAY IT: BASS-kyoo-lin
POKÉDEX NUMBER: 056
TYPE: Water
ABILITY: Reckless/Adaptability
HEIGHT: 3' 03"
WEIGHT: 39.7 lbs.

POSSIBLE MOVES: Tackle, Water Gun, Uproar, Headbutt, Bite, Aqua Jet, Chip Away, Take Down, Crunch, Aqua Tail, Soak, Double-Edge, Scary Face, Flail, Final Gambit, Thrash

Blue-Striped Form

DOES NOT EVOLVE

POKÉMON BLACK VERSION: Red and blue Basculin get along so poorly, they'll start fighting instantly. These Pokémon are very hostile.

POKÉMON WHITE VERSION: Red and blue Basculin usually do not get along, but sometimes members of one school mingle with the other's school.

BEARTIC
FREEZING POKÉMON

HOW TO SAY IT: BAIR-tick
POKÉDEX NUMBER: 120
TYPE: Ice
ABILITY: Snow Cloak
HEIGHT: 8' 06"
WEIGHT: 573.2 lbs.

POSSIBLE MOVES: Superpower, Powder Snow, Growl, Bide, Icy Wind, Growl, Bide, Icy Wind, Fury Swipes, Brine, Endure, Swagger, Slash, Flail, Icicle Crash, Rest, Blizzard, Hail, Thrash, Sheer Cold

Cubchoo → Level 37 → Beartic

EVOLUTIONS

POKÉMON BLACK VERSION: It can make its breath freeze at will. Very able in the water, it swims around in northern seas and catches prey.

POKÉMON WHITE VERSION: It freezes its breath to create fangs and claws of ice to fight with. Cold northern areas are its habitat.

BEHEEYEM
CEREBRAL POKÉMON

HOW TO SAY IT: BEE-hee-ehm
POKÉDEX NUMBER: 112
TYPE: Psychic
ABILITY: Telepathy/Synchronize
HEIGHT: 3' 03"
WEIGHT: 76.1 lbs.

POSSIBLE MOVES: Confusion, Growl, Heal Block, Miracle Eye, Psybeam, Headbutt, Hidden Power, Imprison, Simple Beam, Zen Headbutt, Psych Up, Psychic, Calm Mind, Recover, Guard Split, Power Split, Synchronoise, Wonder Room

Elgyem — Level 42 → Beheeyem

EVOLUTIONS

POKÉMON BLACK VERSION: It can manipulate an opponent's memory. Apparently, it communicates by flashing its three different-colored fingers.

POKÉMON WHITE VERSION: It uses psychic power to control an opponent's brain and tamper with its memories.

BISHARP
SWORD BLADE POKÉMON

HOW TO SAY IT: BIH-sharp
POKÉDEX NUMBER: 131
TYPE: Dark-Steel
ABILITY: Defiant/Inner Focus
HEIGHT: 5' 03"
WEIGHT: 154.3 lbs.

POSSIBLE MOVES: Metal Burst, Scratch, Leer, Fury Cutter, Torment, Faint Attack, Scary Face, Metal Claw, Slash, Assurance, Metal Sound, Embargo, Iron Defense, Night Slash, Iron Head, Swords Dance, Guillotine

Pawniard — Level 52 → Bisharp

EVOLUTIONS

POKÉMON BLACK VERSION: It leads a group of Pawniard. It battles to become the boss, but will be driven from the group if it loses.

POKÉMON WHITE VERSION: Bisharp pursues prey in the company of a large group of Pawniard. Then Bisharp finishes off the prey.

BLITZLE
ELECTRIFIED POKÉMON

HOW TO SAY IT: BLIT-zul
POKÉDEX NUMBER: 028
TYPE: Electric
ABILITY: Lightningrod/Motor Drive
HEIGHT: 2' 07"
WEIGHT: 65.7 lbs.

POSSIBLE MOVES: Quick Attack, Tail Whip, Charge, Shock Wave, Thunder Wave, Flame Charge, Pursuit, Spark, Stomp, Discharge, Agility, Wild Charge, Thrash

Blitzle → Level 27 → Zebstrika

EVOLUTIONS

POKÉMON BLACK VERSION: Its mane shines when it discharges electricity. They use their flashing manes to communicate with one another.

POKÉMON WHITE VERSION: When thunderclouds cover the sky, it will appear. It can catch lightning with its mane and store the electricity.

BOLDORE
ORE POKÉMON

HOW TO SAY IT: BOHL-dohr
POKÉDEX NUMBER: 031
TYPE: Rock
ABILITY: Sturdy
HEIGHT: 2' 11"
WEIGHT: 224.9 lbs.

POSSIBLE MOVES: Tackle, Harden, Sand-Attack, Headbutt, Rock Blast, Mud-Slap, Iron Defense, Smack Down, Power Gem, Rock Slide, Stealth Rock, Sandstorm, Stone Edge, Explosion

POKÉMON BLACK VERSION: When it overflows with power, the orange crystal on its body glows. It looks for underground water in caves.

POKÉMON WHITE VERSION: Because its energy was too great to be contained, the energy leaked and formed orange crystals.

Roggenrola → Level 25 → Boldore → Link Trade → Gigalith

EVOLUTIONS

BOUFFALANT
BASH BUFFALO POKÉMON

HOW TO SAY IT: BOO-fuh-lahnt
POKÉDEX NUMBER: 132
TYPE: Normal
ABILITY: Reckless/Sap Sipper
HEIGHT: 5' 03"
WEIGHT: 208.6 lbs.

POSSIBLE MOVES: Pursuit, Leer, Rage, Fury Attack, Horn Attack, Scary Face, Revenge, Head Charge, Focus Energy, Megahorn, Reversal, Thrash, Swords Dance, Giga Impact

DOES NOT EVOLVE

POKÉMON BLACK VERSION: Their fluffy fur absorbs damage, even if they strike foes with a fierce headbutt.

POKÉMON WHITE VERSION: They charge wildly and headbutt everything. Their headbutts have enough destructive force to derail a train.

BRAVIARY
VALIANT POKÉMON

HOW TO SAY IT: BRAY-vee-air-ee
POKÉDEX NUMBER: 134
TYPE: Normal-Flying
ABILITY: Keen Eye/Sheer Force
HEIGHT: 4' 11"
WEIGHT: 90.4 lbs.

POSSIBLE MOVES: Peck, Leer, Fury Attack, Wing Attack, Hone Claws, Scary Face, Aerial Ace, Slash, Defog, Tailwind, Air Slash, Crush Claw, Sky Drop, Superpower, Whirlwind, Brave Bird, Thrash

Rufflet — Level 54 — **Braviary**
EVOLUTIONS

POKÉMON BLACK VERSION: They fight for their friends without any thought about danger to themselves. One can carry a car while flying.

POKÉMON WHITE VERSION: The more scars they have, the more respect these brave soldiers of the sky get from their peers.

CARRACOSTA
PROTOTURTLE POKÉMON

HOW TO SAY IT: kair-rah-KOSS-tah
POKÉDEX NUMBER: 071
TYPE: Water-Rock
ABILITY: Solid Rock/Sturdy
HEIGHT: 3' 11"
WEIGHT: 178.6 lbs.

POSSIBLE MOVES: Bide, Withdraw, Water Gun, Rollout, Bite, Protect, Aqua Jet, AncientPower, Crunch, Wide Guard, Brine, Smack Down, Curse, Shell Smash, Aqua Tail, Rock Slide, Rain Dance, Hydro Pump

Tirtouga → Level 37 → Carracosta

EVOLUTIONS

POKÉMON BLACK VERSION: They can live both in the ocean and on land. A slap from one of them is enough to open a hole in the bottom of a tanker.

POKÉMON WHITE VERSION: Incredible jaw strength enables them to chew up steel beams and rocks along with their prey.

CHANDELURE
LURING POKÉMON

HOW TO SAY IT: shan-duh-LOOR
POKÉDEX NUMBER: 115
TYPE: Ghost-Fire
ABILITY: Flash Fire/Flame Body
HEIGHT: 3' 03"
WEIGHT: 75.6 lbs.

POSSIBLE MOVES: Smog, Confuse Ray, Flame Burst, Hex

POKÉMON BLACK VERSION: It absorbs a spirit, which it then burns. By waving the flames on its arms, it puts its foes into a hypnotic trance.

POKÉMON WHITE VERSION: Being consumed in Chandelure's flame burns up the spirit, leaving the body behind.

Litwick → Level 41 → Lampent → Dusk Stone → Chandelure

EVOLUTIONS

CINCCINO
SCARF POKÉMON

HOW TO SAY IT: chin-CHEE-noh
POKÉDEX NUMBER: 079
TYPE: Normal
ABILITY: Cute Charm/Technician
HEIGHT: 1' 08"
WEIGHT: 16.5 lbs.
POSSIBLE MOVES: Bullet Seed, Rock Blast, Helping Hand, Tickle, Sing, Tail Slap

POKÉMON BLACK VERSION: Their white fur is coated in a special oil that makes it easy for them to deflect attacks.

POKÉMON WHITE VERSION: Their white fur feels amazing to touch. Their fur repels dust and prevents static electricity from building up.

Minccino → Shiny Stone → Cinccino

EVOLUTIONS

COBALION
IRON WILL POKÉMON

HOW TO SAY IT: koh-BAY-lee-un
POKÉDEX NUMBER: 144
TYPE: Steel-Fighting
ABILITY: Justified
HEIGHT: 6' 11"
WEIGHT: 551.2 lbs.

POSSIBLE MOVES: Quick Attack, Leer, Double Kick, Metal Claw, Take Down, Helping Hand, Retaliate, Iron Head, Sacred Sword, Swords Dance, Quick Guard, Work Up, Metal Burst, Close Combat

LEGENDARY POKÉMON

POKÉMON BLACK VERSION: This legendary Pokémon battled against humans to protect Pokémon. Its personality is calm and composed.

POKÉMON WHITE VERSION: It has a body and heart of steel. Its glare is sufficient to make even an unruly Pokémon obey it.

DOES NOT EVOLVE

COFAGRIGUS
COFFIN POKÉMON

HOW TO SAY IT: kof-uh-GREE-guss
POKÉDEX NUMBER: 069
TYPE: Ghost
ABILITY: Mummy
HEIGHT: 5' 07"
WEIGHT: 168.7 lbs.

POSSIBLE MOVES: Astonish, Protect, Disable, Haze, Night Shade, Hex, Will-O-Wisp, Ominous Wind, Curse, Power Split, Guard Split, Scary Face, Shadow Ball, Grudge, Mean Look, Destiny Bond

Yamask → Level 34 → Cofagrigus
EVOLUTIONS

POKÉMON BLACK VERSION: It has been said that they swallow those who get too close and turn them into mummies. They like to eat gold nuggets.

POKÉMON WHITE VERSION: They pretend to be elaborate coffins to teach lessons to grave robbers. Their bodies are covered in pure gold.

CONKELDURR
MUSCULAR POKÉMON

HOW TO SAY IT: kon-KELL-dur
POKÉDEX NUMBER: 040
TYPE: Fighting
ABILITY: Guts/Sheer Force
HEIGHT: 4' 07"
WEIGHT: 191.8 lbs.

POSSIBLE MOVES: Pound, Leer, Focus Energy, Bide, Low Kick, Rock Throw, Wake-Up Slap, Chip Away, Bulk Up, Rock Slide, DynamicPunch, Scary Face, Hammer Arm, Stone Edge, Focus Punch, Superpower

POKÉMON BLACK VERSION: It is thought that Conkeldurr taught humans how to make concrete more than 2,000 years ago.

POKÉMON WHITE VERSION: They use concrete pillars as walking canes. They know moves that enable them to swing the pillars freely in battle.

Timburr → Level 25 → Gurdurr → Link Trade → Conkeldurr
EVOLUTIONS

COTTONEE
COTTON PUFF POKÉMON

HOW TO SAY IT: KAHT-ton-ee
POKÉDEX NUMBER: 052
TYPE: Grass
ABILITY: Prankster/Infiltrator
HEIGHT: 1' 00"
WEIGHT: 1.3 lbs.

POSSIBLE MOVES: Absorb, Growth, Leech Seed, Stun Spore, Mega Drain, Cotton Spore, Razor Leaf, PoisonPowder, Giga Drain, Charm, Helping Hand, Energy Ball, Cotton Guard, Sunny Day, Endeavor, SolarBeam

Cottonee → Sun Stone → Whimsicott
EVOLUTIONS

POKÉMON BLACK VERSION: When attacked, it escapes by shooting cotton from its body. The cotton serves as a decoy to distract the attacker.

POKÉMON WHITE VERSION: They go wherever the wind takes them. On rainy days, their bodies are heavier, so they take shelter beneath big trees.

CRUSTLE
STONE HOME POKÉMON

HOW TO SAY IT: KRUS-tul
POKÉDEX NUMBER: 064
TYPE: Bug-Rock
ABILITY: Sturdy/Shell Armor
HEIGHT: 4' 07"
WEIGHT: 440.9 lbs.

POSSIBLE MOVES: Shell Smash, Rock Blast, Withdraw, Sand-Attack, Faint Attack, Smack Down, Rock Polish, Bug Bite, Stealth Rock, Rock Slide, Slash, X-Scissor, Shell Smash, Flail, Rock Wrecker

Dwebble → Level 34 → Crustle
EVOLUTIONS

POKÉMON BLACK VERSION: Competing for territory, Crustle fight viciously. The one whose boulder is broken is the loser of the battle.

POKÉMON WHITE VERSION: It possesses legs of enormou strength, enabling it to carry heavy slabs for many days, even when crossing arid land.

CRYOGONAL
CRYSTALLIZING POKÉMON

HOW TO SAY IT: kry-AH-guh-nul
POKÉDEX NUMBER: 121
TYPE: Ice
ABILITY: Levitate
HEIGHT: 3' 07"
WEIGHT: 326.3 lbs.

POSSIBLE MOVES: Bind, Ice Shard, Sharpen, Rapid Spin, Icy Wind, Mist, Haze, Aurora Beam, Acid Armor, Ice Beam, Light Screen, Reflect, Slash, Confuse Ray, Recover, SolarBeam, Night Slash, Sheer Cold

POKÉMON BLACK VERSION:
When its body temperature goes up, it turns into steam and vanishes. When its temperature lowers, it returns to ice.

POKÉMON WHITE VERSION:
They are born in snow clouds. They use chains made of ice crystals to capture prey.

DOES NOT EVOLVE

CUBCHOO
CHILL POKÉMON

HOW TO SAY IT: cub-CHOO
POKÉDEX NUMBER: 119
TYPE: Ice
ABILITY: Snow Cloak
HEIGHT: 1' 08"
WEIGHT: 18.7 lbs.

POSSIBLE MOVES: Powder Snow, Growl, Bide, Icy Wind, Fury Swipes, Brine, Endure, Charm, Slash, Flail, Rest, Blizzard, Hail, Thrash, Sheer Cold

POKÉMON BLACK VERSION:
When it is not feeling well, its mucus gets watery and the power of its Ice-type moves decreases.

POKÉMON WHITE VERSION:
Its nose is always running. It sniffs the snot back up because the mucus provides the raw material for its moves.

Cubchoo — Level 37 → Beartic

EVOLUTIONS

DARMANITAN
BLAZING POKÉMON

HOW TO SAY IT: dar-MAN-ih-tan
POKÉDEX NUMBER: 061
TYPE: Fire
ABILITY: Sheer Force
HEIGHT: 4' 03"
WEIGHT: 204.8 lbs.
POSSIBLE MOVES: Tackle, Rollout, Incinerate, Rage, Fire Fang, Headbutt, Swagger, Facade, Fire Punch, Work Up, Thrash, Belly Drum, Flare Blitz, Hammer Arm, Taunt, Superpower, Overheat

Level 35

Darumaka → **Darmanitan**
EVOLUTIONS

POKÉMON BLACK VERSION:
Its internal fire burns at 2,500° F, making enough power that it can destroy a dump truck with one punch.

POKÉMON WHITE VERSION:
When weakened in battle, it transforms into a stone statue. Then it sharpens its mind and fights on mentally.

DARUMAKA
ZEN CHARM POKÉMON

HOW TO SAY IT: dah-roo-MAH-kuh
POKÉDEX NUMBER: 060
TYPE: Fire
ABILITY: Hustle
HEIGHT: 2' 00"
WEIGHT: 82.7 lbs.
POSSIBLE MOVES: Tackle, Rollout, Incinerate, Rage, Fire Fang, Headbutt, Uproar, Facade, Fire Punch, Work Up, Thrash, Belly Drum, Flare Blitz, Taunt, Superpower, Overheat

Level 35

Darumaka → **Darmanitan**
EVOLUTIONS

POKÉMON BLACK VERSION:
When its internal fire is burning, it cannot calm down and it runs around. When the fire diminishes, it falls asleep.

POKÉMON WHITE VERSION:
Darumaka's droppings are hot, so people used to put them in their clothes to keep themselves warm.

DEERLING
SEASON POKÉMON

Spring Form

HOW TO SAY IT: DEER-ling
POKÉDEX NUMBER: 091
TYPE: Normal-Grass
ABILITY: Chlorophyll/Sap Sipper
HEIGHT: 2' 00"
WEIGHT: 43.0 lbs.
POSSIBLE MOVES: Tackle, Camouflage, Growl, Sand-Attack, Double Kick, Leech Seed, Faint Attack, Take Down, Jump Kick, Aromatherapy, Energy Ball, Charm, Nature Power, Double-Edge, SolarBeam

Summer Form

Autumn Form

Winter Form

POKÉMON BLACK VERSION:
The color and scent of their fur changes to match the mountain grass. When they sense hostility, they hide in the grass.

POKÉMON WHITE VERSION:
The turning of the seasons changes the color and scent of this Pokémon's fur. People use it to mark the seasons.

Deerling → Level 34 → Sawsbuck
EVOLUTIONS

DEINO
IRATE POKÉMON

HOW TO SAY IT: DY-noh
POKÉDEX NUMBER: 139
TYPE: Dark-Dragon
ABILITY: Hustle
HEIGHT: 2' 07"
WEIGHT: 38.1 lbs.
POSSIBLE MOVES: Tackle, Dragon Rage, Focus Energy, Bite, Headbutt, DragonBreath, Roar, Crunch, Slam, Dragon Pulse, Work Up, Dragon Rush, Body Slam, Scary Face, Hyper Voice, Outrage

POKÉMON BLACK VERSION: It tends to bite everything, and it is not a picky eater. Approaching it carelessly is dangerous.

POKÉMON WHITE VERSION: They cannot see, so they tackl and bite to learn about their surroundings. Their bodies are covered in wounds.

Deino → Level 50 → Zweilous → Level 64 → Hydreigon

EVOLUTIONS

DEWOTT
DISCIPLINE POKÉMON

HOW TO SAY IT: DOO-wot
POKÉDEX NUMBER: 008
TYPE: Water
ABILITY: Torrent
HEIGHT: 2' 07"
WEIGHT: 54.0 lbs.
POSSIBLE MOVES: Tackle, Tail Whip, Water Gun, Water Sport, Focus Energy, Razor Shell, Fury Cutter, Water Pulse, Revenge, Aqua Jet, Encore, Aqua Tail, Retaliate, Swords Dance, Hydro Pump

What's a scalchop? Turn to page 59 to find out!

POKÉMON BLACK VERSION: Strict training is how it learns its flowing double-scalchop technique.

POKÉMON WHITE VERSIO Scalchop techniques differ from one Dewott to another It never neglects maintainin its scalchops.

Oshawott → Level 17 → Dewott → Level 36 → Samurott

EVOLUTIONS

DRILBUR
MOLE POKÉMON

HOW TO SAY IT: DRIL-bur
POKÉDEX NUMBER: 035
TYPE: Ground
ABILITY: Sand Rush/Sand Force
HEIGHT: 1' 00"
WEIGHT: 18.7 lbs.

POSSIBLE MOVES: Scratch, Mud Sport, Rapid Spin, Mud-Slap, Fury Swipes, Metal Claw, Dig, Hone Claws, Slash, Rock Slide, Earthquake, Swords Dance, Sandstorm, Drill Run, Fissure

 Level 31

Drilbur   **Excadrill**
EVOLUTIONS

POKÉMON BLACK VERSION:
It can dig through the ground at a speed of 30 mph. It could give a car running aboveground a good race.

POKÉMON WHITE VERSION:
It makes its way swiftly through the soil by putting both claws together and rotating at high speed.

DRUDDIGON
CAVE POKÉMON

HOW TO SAY IT: DRUD-dih-gahn
POKÉDEX NUMBER: 127
TYPE: Dragon
ABILITY: Rough Skin/Sheer Force
HEIGHT: 5' 03"
WEIGHT: 306.4 lbs.

POSSIBLE MOVES: Leer, Scratch, Hone Claws, Bite, Scary Face, Dragon Rage, Slash, Crunch, Dragon Claw, Chip Away, Revenge, Night Slash, Dragon Tail, Rock Climb, Superpower, Outrage

DOES NOT EVOLVE

POKÉMON BLACK VERSION:
It warms its body by absorbing sunlight with its wings. When its body temperature falls, it can no longer move.

POKÉMON WHITE VERSION:
It races through narrow caves, using its sharp claws to catch prey. The skin on its face is harder than a rock.

DUCKLETT
WATER BIRD POKÉMON

HOW TO SAY IT: DUK-lit
POKÉDEX NUMBER: 086
TYPE: Water-Flying
ABILITY: Keen Eye/Big Pecks
HEIGHT: 1' 08"
WEIGHT: 12.1 lbs.
POSSIBLE MOVES: Water Gun, Water Sport, Defog, Wing Attack, Water Pulse, Aerial Ace, BubbleBeam, FeatherDance, Aqua Ring, Air Slash, Roost, Rain Dance, Tailwind, Brave Bird, Hurricane

Ducklett **Level 35** Swanna

EVOLUTIONS

POKÉMON BLACK VERSION: These bird Pokémon are excellent divers. They swim around in the water eating their favorite food – peat moss.

POKÉMON WHITE VERSION: When attacked, it uses its feathers to splash water, escaping under cover of the spray.

DUOSION
MITOSIS POKÉMON

HOW TO SAY IT: doo-OH-zhun
POKÉDEX NUMBER: 084
TYPE: Psychic
ABILITY: Overcoat/Magic Guard
HEIGHT: 2' 00"
WEIGHT: 17.6 lbs.
POSSIBLE MOVES: Psywave, Reflect, Rollout, Snatch, Hidden Power, Light Screen, Charm, Recover, Psyshock, Endeavor, Future Sight, Pain Split, Psychic, Skill Swap, Heal Block, Wonder Room

Solosis **Level 32** Duosion **Level 41** Reuniclus

EVOLUTIONS

POKÉMON BLACK VERSION: Since they have two divided brains, at times they suddenly try to take two different actions at once.

POKÉMON WHITE VERSION: When their brains, now divided in two, are thinking the same thoughts, these Pokémon exhibit their maximum power.

DURANT
IRON ANT POKÉMON

HOW TO SAY IT: dur-ANT
POKÉDEX NUMBER: 138
TYPE: Bug-Steel
ABILITY: Swarm/Hustle
HEIGHT: 1' 00"
WEIGHT: 72.8 lbs.
POSSIBLE MOVES:
ViceGrip, Sand-Attack,
Fury Cutter, Bite, Agility,
Metal Claw, Bug Bite, Crunch, Iron
Head, Dig, Entrainment, X-Scissor,
Iron Defense, Guillotine,
Metal Sound

POKÉMON BLACK VERSION:
They attack in groups, covering
themselves in steel armor
to protect themselves from
Heatmor.

POKÉMON WHITE VERSION:
Durant dig nests in mountains.
They build their complicated,
interconnected tunnels into
mazes.

DOES NOT EVOLVE

DWEBBLE
ROCK INN POKÉMON

HOW TO SAY IT: DWEHB-bul
POKÉDEX NUMBER: 063
TYPE: Bug-Rock
ABILITY: Sturdy/Shell Armor
HEIGHT: 1' 00"
WEIGHT: 32.0 lbs.
POSSIBLE MOVES: Fury Cutter, Rock
Blast, Withdraw, Sand-Attack, Faint
Attack, Smack Down, Rock Polish, Bug Bite,
Stealth Rock, Rock Slide, Slash, X-Scissor,
Shell Smash, Flail, Rock Wrecker

POKÉMON BLACK VERSION:
This Pokémon can easily melt
holes in hard rocks with a liquid
secreted from its mouth.

POKÉMON WHITE VERSION:
It makes a hole in a suitable
rock. If that rock breaks, the
Pokémon remains agitated
until it locates a replacement.

Level 34
Dwebble → Crustle
EVOLUTIONS

EELEKTRIK

ELEFISH POKÉMON

HOW TO SAY IT: ee-LEK-trik
POKÉDEX NUMBER: 109
TYPE: Electric
ABILITY: Levitate
HEIGHT: 3' 11"
WEIGHT: 48.5 lbs.
POSSIBLE MOVES: Headbutt, Thunder Wave, Spark, Charge Beam, Bind, Acid, Discharge, Crunch, Thunderbolt, Acid Spray, Coil, Wild Charge, Gastro Acid, Zap Cannon, Thrash

Tynamo — Level 39 → Eelektrik — Thunderstone → Eelektross

EVOLUTIONS

POKÉMON BLACK VERSION: They coil around foes and shock them with electricity-generating organs that seem simply to be circular patterns.

POKÉMON WHITE VERSION: These Pokémon have a big appetite. When they spot their prey, they attack it and paralyze it with electricity.

EELEKTROSS

ELEFISH POKÉMON

HOW TO SAY IT: ee-LEK-trahs
POKÉDEX NUMBER: 110
TYPE: Electric
ABILITY: Levitate
HEIGHT: 6' 11"
WEIGHT: 177.5 lbs.
POSSIBLE MOVES: Crush Claw, Headbutt, Acid, Discharge, Crunch

POKÉMON BLACK VERSION: They crawl out of the ocean using their arms. They will attack prey on shore and immediately drag it into the ocean.

POKÉMON WHITE VERSION: With their sucker mouths, they suck in prey. Then they use their fangs to shock the prey with electricity.

Tynamo — Level 39 → Eelektrik — Thunderstone → Eelektross

EVOLUTIONS

ELGYEM
CEREBRAL POKÉMON

HOW TO SAY IT: ELL-jee-ehm
POKÉDEX NUMBER: 111
TYPE: Psychic
ABILITY: Telepathy/Synchronize
HEIGHT: 1' 08"
WEIGHT: 19.8 lbs.
POSSIBLE MOVES: Confusion, Growl, Heal Block, Miracle Eye, Psybeam, Headbutt, Hidden Power, Imprison, Simple Beam, Zen Headbutt, Psych Up, Psychic, Calm Mind, Recover, Guard Split, Power Split, Synchronoise, Wonder Room

POKÉMON BLACK VERSION: It uses its strong psychic power to squeeze its opponent's brain, causing unendurable headaches.

POKÉMON WHITE VERSION: This Pokémon had never been seen until it appeared from far in the desert 50 years ago.

Elgyem → Level 42 → Beheeyem

EVOLUTIONS

EMBOAR
MEGA FIRE PIG POKÉMON

HOW TO SAY IT: EHM-bohr
POKÉDEX NUMBER: 006
TYPE: Fire-Fighting
ABILITY: Blaze
HEIGHT: 5' 03"
WEIGHT: 330.7 lbs.

POSSIBLE MOVES: Hammer Arm, Tackle, Tail Whip, Ember, Odor Sleuth, Defense Curl, Flame Charge, Arm Thrust, Smog, Rollout, Take Down, Heat Crash, Assurance, Flamethrower, Head Smash, Roar, Flare Blitz

Tepig → Level 17 → Pignite → Level 36 → Emboar

EVOLUTIONS

POKÉMON BLACK VERSION: It can throw a fire punch by setting its fists on fire with its fiery chin. It cares deeply about its friends.

POKÉMON WHITE VERSION: It has mastered fast and powerful fighting moves. It grows a beard of fire.

EMOLGA
SKY SQUIRREL POKÉMON

HOW TO SAY IT: ee-MAHL-guh
POKÉDEX NUMBER: 093
TYPE: Electric-Flying
ABILITY: Static
HEIGHT: 1' 04"
WEIGHT: 11.0 lbs.

POSSIBLE MOVES: ThunderShock, Quick Attack, Tail Whip, Charge, Spark, Pursuit, Double Team, Shock Wave, Electro Ball, Acrobatics, Light Screen, Encore, Volt Switch, Agility, Discharge

POKÉMON BLACK VERSION: The energy made in its cheeks' electric pouches is stored inside its membrane and released while it is gliding.

POKÉMON WHITE VERSION: They live on treetops and glide using the inside of a cape-like membrane while discharging electricity.

DOES NOT EVOLVE

ESCAVALIER
CAVALRY POKÉMON

HOW TO SAY IT: ess-KAH-vuh-LEER
POKÉDEX NUMBER: 095
TYPE: Bug-Steel
ABILITY: Swarm/Shell Armor
HEIGHT: 3' 03"
WEIGHT: 72.8 lbs.

POSSIBLE MOVES: Peck, Leer, Quick Guard, Twineedle, Fury Attack, Headbutt, False Swipe, Bug Buzz, Slash, Iron Head, Iron Defense, X-Scissor, Reversal, Swords Dance, Giga Impact

Link Trade Shelmet and Karrablast →

Karrablast   **Escavalier**
EVOLUTIONS

POKÉMON BLACK VERSION:
They fly around at high speed, striking with their pointed spears. Even when in trouble, they face opponents bravely.

POKÉMON WHITE VERSION:
These Pokémon evolve by wearing the shell covering of a Shelmet. The steel armor protects their whole body.

EXCADRILL
SUBTERRENE POKÉMON

HOW TO SAY IT: EKS-kuh-dril
POKÉDEX NUMBER: 036
TYPE: Ground-Steel
ABILITY: Sand Rush/Sand Force
HEIGHT: 2' 04"
WEIGHT: 89.1 lbs.

POSSIBLE MOVES: Scratch, Mud Sport, Rapid Spin, Mud-Slap, Fury Swipes, Metal Claw, Dig, Hone Claws, Slash, Rock Slide, Horn Drill, Earthquake, Swords Dance, Sandstorm, Drill Run, Fissure

Level 31

Drilbur   **Excadrill**
EVOLUTIONS

POKÉMON BLACK VERSION:
It can help in tunnel construction. Its drill has evolved into steel strong enough to bore through iron plates.

POKÉMON WHITE VERSION:
More than 300 feet below the surface, they build mazelike nests. Their activity can be destructive to subway tunnels.

FERROSEED
THORN SEED POKÉMON

HOW TO SAY IT: fer-AH-seed
POKÉDEX NUMBER: 103
TYPE: Grass-Steel
ABILITY: Iron Barbs
HEIGHT: 2' 00"
WEIGHT: 41.4 lbs.
POSSIBLE MOVES: Tackle, Harden, Rollout, Curse, Metal Claw, Pin Missile, Gyro Ball, Iron Defense, Mirror Shot, Ingrain, Selfdestruct, Iron Head, Payback, Flash Cannon, Explosion

Ferroseed → Level 40 → Ferrothorn
EVOLUTIONS

POKÉMON BLACK VERSION:
When threatened, it attacks by shooting a barrage of spikes, which gives it a chance to escape by rolling away.

POKÉMON WHITE VERSION:
They stick their spikes into cave walls and absorb the minerals they find in the rock

FERROTHORN
THORN POD POKÉMON

HOW TO SAY IT: fer-AH-thorn
POKÉDEX NUMBER: 104
TYPE: Grass-Steel
ABILITY: Iron Barbs
HEIGHT: 3' 03"
WEIGHT: 242.5 lbs.
POSSIBLE MOVES: Rock Climb, Tackle, Harden, Rollout, Curse, Metal Claw, Pin Missile, Gyro Ball, Iron Defense, Mirror Shot, Ingrain, Selfdestruct, Power Whip, Iron Head, Payback, Flash Cannon, Explosion

Ferroseed → Level 40 → Ferrothorn
EVOLUTIONS

POKÉMON BLACK VERSION:
It fights by swinging around its three spiky feelers. A hit from these steel spikes can reduce a boulder to rubble.

POKÉMON WHITE VERSION:
They attach themselves to cave ceilings, firing steel spikes at targets passing beneath them

FOONGUS
MUSHROOM POKÉMON

HOW TO SAY IT: FOON-gus
POKÉDEX NUMBER: 096
TYPE: Grass-Poison
ABILITY: Effect Spore
HEIGHT: 0' 08"
WEIGHT: 2.2 lbs.
POSSIBLE MOVES: Absorb, Growth, Astonish,
Bide, Mega Drain, Ingrain, Faint Attack,
Sweet Scent, Giga Drain, Toxic, Synthesis,
Clear Smog, SolarBeam, Rage Powder,
Spore

Foongus →Level 39→ Amoonguss

EVOLUTIONS

POKÉMON BLACK VERSION:
It lures people in with its Poké
Ball pattern, then releases
poison spores. Why It resembles
a Poké Ball is unknown.

POKÉMON WHITE VERSION:
For some reason, this Pokémon
resembles a Poké Ball. They
release poison spores to repel
those who try to catch them.

FRAXURE
AXE JAW POKÉMON

HOW TO SAY IT: FRAK-shur
POKÉDEX NUMBER: 117
TYPE: Dragon
ABILITY: Rivalry/Mold Breaker
HEIGHT: 3' 03"
WEIGHT: 79.4 lbs.
POSSIBLE MOVES: Scratch, Leer, Assurance,
Dragon Rage, Dual Chop, Scary Face,
Slash, False Swipe, Dragon Claw,
Dragon Dance, Taunt, Dragon
Pulse, Swords Dance, Guillotine,
Outrage, Giga Impact

POKÉMON BLACK VERSION:
Since a broken tusk will not grow
back, they diligently sharpen
their tusks on river rocks after
they've been fighting.

POKÉMON WHITE VERSION:
Their tusks can shatter rocks.
Territory battles between
Fraxure can be intensely
violent.

Axew →Level 38→ Fraxure →Level 48→ Haxorus

EVOLUTIONS

FRILLISH
FLOATING POKÉMON

HOW TO SAY IT: FRIL-lish
POKÉDEX NUMBER: 098
TYPE: Water-Ghost
ABILITY: Water Absorb/Cursed Body
HEIGHT: 3' 11"
WEIGHT: 72.8 lbs.

POSSIBLE MOVES: Bubble, Water Sport, Absorb, Night Shade, BubbleBeam, Recover, Water Pulse, Ominous Wind, Brine, Rain Dance, Hex, Hydro Pump, Wring Out, Water Spout

Frillish ♂

Frillish ♀

Frillish → Level 40 → **Jellicent**
EVOLUTIONS

POKÉMON BLACK VERSION: With its thin, veil-like arms wrapped around the body of its opponent, it sinks to the ocean floor.

POKÉMON WHITE VERSION: They paralyze prey with poison, then drag them down to their lairs, five miles below the surface.

GALVANTULA
ELESPIDER POKÉMON

HOW TO SAY IT: gal-VAN-choo-luh
POKÉDEX NUMBER: 102
TYPE: Bug-Electric
ABILITY: Compoundeyes/Unnerve
HEIGHT: 2' 07"
WEIGHT: 31.5 lbs.

POSSIBLE MOVES: String Shot, Leech Life, Spider Web, Thunder Wave, Screech, Fury Cutter, Electroweb, Bug Bite, Gastro Acid, Slash, Electro Ball, Signal Beam, Agility, Sucker Punch, Discharge, Bug Buzz

Joltik → Level 36 → **Galvantula**
EVOLUTIONS

POKÉMON BLACK VERSION: When attacked, they create an electric barrier by spitting out many electrically charged threads.

POKÉMON WHITE VERSION: They employ an electrically charged web to trap their prey. While it is immobilized by shock, they leisurely consume it.

GARBODOR
TRASH HEAP POKÉMON

HOW TO SAY IT: gar-BOH-dur
POKÉDEX NUMBER: 075
TYPE: Poison
ABILITY: Stench/Weak Armor
HEIGHT: 6' 03"
WEIGHT: 236.6 lbs.
POSSIBLE MOVES: Pound, Poison Gas, Recycle, Toxic Spikes, Acid Spray, DoubleSlap, Sludge, Stockpile, Swallow, Body Slam, Sludge Bomb, Clear Smog, Toxic, Amnesia, Gunk Shot, Explosion

POKÉMON BLACK VERSION: It clenches opponents with its left arm and finishes them off with foul-smelling poison gas belched from its mouth.

POKÉMON WHITE VERSION: They absorb garbage and make it part of their bodies. They shoot a poisonous liquid from their right-hand fingertips.

Trubbish → Level 36 → Garbodor
EVOLUTIONS

GIGALITH
COMPRESSED POKÉMON

HOW TO SAY IT: GIH-gah-lith
POKÉDEX NUMBER: 032
TYPE: Rock
ABILITY: Sturdy
HEIGHT: 5' 07"
WEIGHT: 573.2 lbs.
POSSIBLE MOVES: Tackle, Harden, Sand-Attack, Headbutt, Rock Blast, Mud-Slap, Iron Defense, Smack Down, Power Gem, Rock Slide, Stealth Rock, Sandstorm, Stone Edge, Explosion

POKÉMON BLACK VERSION: Compressing the energy from its internal core lets it fire off an attack capable of blowing away a mountain.

POKÉMON WHITE VERSION: The solar energy absorbed by its body's orange crystals is magnified internally and fired from its mouth.

Roggenrola → Level 25 → Boldore → Link Trade → Gigalith
EVOLUTIONS

GOLETT
AUTOMATON POKÉMON

HOW TO SAY IT: GO-let
POKÉDEX NUMBER: 128
TYPE: Ground-Ghost
ABILITY: Iron Fist/Klutz
HEIGHT: 3' 03"
WEIGHT: 202.8 lbs.
POSSIBLE MOVES: Pound, Astonish, Defense Curl, Mud-Slap, Rollout, Shadow Punch, Iron Defense, Mega Punch, Magnitude, DynamicPunch, Night Shade, Curse, Earthquake, Hammer Arm, Focus Punch

Golett → Level 43 → Golurk
EVOLUTIONS

POKÉMON BLACK VERSION: The energy that burns inside it enables it to move, but no one has yet been able to identify this energy.

POKÉMON WHITE VERSION: These Pokémon are thought to have been created by the science of an ancient and mysterious civilization.

GOLURK
AUTOMATON POKÉMON

HOW TO SAY IT: GO-lurk
POKÉDEX NUMBER: 129
TYPE: Ground-Ghost
ABILITY: Iron Fist/Klutz
HEIGHT: 9' 02"
WEIGHT: 727.5 lbs.
POSSIBLE MOVES: Pound, Astonish, Defense Curl, Mud-Slap, Rollout, Shadow Punch, Iron Defense, Mega Punch, Magnitude, DynamicPunch, Night Shade, Curse, Heavy Slam, Earthquake, Hammer Arm, Focus Punch

Golett → Level 43 → Golurk
EVOLUTIONS

POKÉMON BLACK VERSION: It flies across the sky at Mach speeds. Removing the seal on its chest makes its internal energy go out of control.

POKÉMON WHITE VERSION: It is said that Golurk were ordered to protect people and Pokémon by the ancient people who made them.

GOTHITA
FIXATION POKÉMON

HOW TO SAY IT: GAH-THEE-tah

POKÉDEX NUMBER: 080

TYPE: Psychic

ABILITY: Frisk

HEIGHT: 1' 04"

WEIGHT: 12.8 lbs.

POSSIBLE MOVES: Pound, Confusion, Tickle, Fake Tears, DoubleSlap, Psybeam, Embargo, Faint Attack, Psyshock, Flatter, Future Sight, Heal Block, Psychic, Telekinesis, Charm, Magic Room

POKÉMON BLACK VERSION:
Their ribbonlike feelers increase their psychic power. They are always staring at something.

POKÉMON WHITE VERSION:
They intently observe both Trainers and Pokémon. Apparently, they are looking at something that only Gothita can see.

Gothita → Level 32 → Gothorita → Level 41 → Gothitelle

EVOLUTIONS

GOTHITELLE
ASTRAL BODY POKÉMON

HOW TO SAY IT: GAH-thih-tell
POKÉDEX NUMBER: 082
TYPE: Psychic
ABILITY: Frisk
HEIGHT: 4' 11"
WEIGHT: 97.0 lbs.

POSSIBLE MOVES: Pound, Confusion, Tickle, Fake Tears, DoubleSlap, Psybeam, Embargo, Faint Attack, Psyshock, Flatter, Future Sight, Heal Block, Psychic, Telekinesis, Charm, Magic Room

POKÉMON BLACK VERSION: Starry skies thousands of light-years away are visible in the space distorted by their intense psychic power.

POKÉMON WHITE VERSION: They can predict the future from the placement and movement of the stars. They can see Trainers' life spans.

Gothita →Level 32→ Gothorita →Level 41→ Gothitelle

EVOLUTIONS

GOTHORITA
MANIPULATE POKÉMON

HOW TO SAY IT: GAH-thoh-REE-tah
POKÉDEX NUMBER: 081
TYPE: Psychic
ABILITY: Frisk
HEIGHT: 2' 04"
WEIGHT: 39.7 lbs.

POSSIBLE MOVES: Pound, Confusion, Tickle, Fake Tears, DoubleSlap, Psybeam, Embargo, Faint Attack, Psyshock, Flatter, Future Sight, Heal Block, Psychic, Telekinesis, Charm, Magic Room

POKÉMON BLACK VERSION: They use hypnosis to control people and Pokémon. Tales of Gothorita leading people astray are told in every corner.

POKÉMON WHITE VERSION: Starlight is the source of their power. At night, they mark star positions by using psychic power to float stones.

Gothita →Level 32→ Gothorita →Level 41→ Gothitelle

EVOLUTIONS

GURDURR
MUSCULAR POKÉMON

HOW TO SAY IT: GUR-dur
POKÉDEX NUMBER: 039
TYPE: Fighting
ABILITY: Guts/Sheer Force
HEIGHT: 3' 11"
WEIGHT: 88.2 lbs.
POSSIBLE MOVES: Pound, Leer, Focus Energy, Bide, Low Kick, Rock Throw, Wake-Up Slap, Chip Away, Bulk Up, Rock Slide, DynamicPunch, Scary Face, Hammer Arm, Stone Edge, Focus Punch, Superpower

POKÉMON BLACK VERSION: This Pokémon is so muscular and strongly built that even a group of wrestlers could not make it budge an inch.

POKÉMON WHITE VERSION: They strengthen their bodies by carrying steel beams. They show off their big muscles to their friends.

Timburr → Level 25 → Gurdurr → Link Trade → Conkeldurr

EVOLUTIONS

HAXORUS
AXE JAW POKÉMON

HOW TO SAY IT: HAK-soar-us
POKÉDEX NUMBER: 118
TYPE: Dragon
ABILITY: Rivalry/Mold Breaker
HEIGHT: 5' 11"
WEIGHT: 232.6 lbs.
POSSIBLE MOVES: Scratch, Leer, Assurance, Dragon Rage, Dual Chop, Scary Face, Slash, False Swipe, Dragon Claw, Dragon Dance, Taunt, Dragon Pulse, Swords Dance, Guillotine, Outrage, Giga Impact

POKÉMON BLACK VERSION: They are kind but can be relentless when defending territory. They challenge foes with tusks that can cut steel.

POKÉMON WHITE VERSION: Their sturdy tusks will stay sharp even if used to cut steel beams. These Pokémon are covered in hard armor.

Axew → Level 38 → Fraxure → Level 48 → Haxorus

EVOLUTIONS

HEATMOR
ANTEATER POKÉMON

HOW TO SAY IT: HEET-mohr
POKÉDEX NUMBER: 137
TYPE: Fire
ABILITY: Gluttony/Flash Fire
HEIGHT: 4' 07"
WEIGHT: 127.9 lbs.
POSSIBLE MOVES: Incinerate, Lick, Odor Sleuth, Bind, Fire Spin, Fury Swipes, Snatch, Flame Burst, Bug Bite, Slash, Amnesia, Flamethrower, Stockpile, Spit Up, Swallow, Inferno

DOES NOT EVOLVE

POKÉMON BLACK VERSION:
It breathes through a hole in its tail while it burns with an internal fire. Durant is its prey.

POKÉMON WHITE VERSION:
Using their very hot, flame-covered tongues, they burn through Durant's steel bodies and consume their insides.

HERDIER
LOYAL DOG POKÉMON

HOW TO SAY IT: HERD-ee-er
POKÉDEX NUMBER: 013
TYPE: Normal
ABILITY: Intimidate/Sand Rush
HEIGHT: 2' 11"
WEIGHT: 32.4 lbs.
POSSIBLE MOVES: Leer, Tackle, Odor Sleuth, Bite, Helping Hand, Take Down, Work Up, Crunch, Roar, Retaliate, Reversal, Last Resort, Giga Impact

POKÉMON BLACK VERSION:
It has black, cape-like fur that is very hard and decreases the amount of damage it receives.

POKÉMON WHITE VERSION:
It loyally follows its Trainer's orders. For ages, they have helped Trainers raise Pokémon.

Level 16 → Level 32

Lillipup   Herdier   Stoutland
EVOLUTIONS

HYDREIGON
BRUTAL POKÉMON

HOW TO SAY IT: hy-DRY-gahn
POKÉDEX NUMBER: 141
TYPE: Dark-Dragon
ABILITY: Levitate
HEIGHT: 5' 11"
WEIGHT: 352.7 lbs.
POSSIBLE MOVES:
Tri Attack, Dragon Rage, Focus Energy, Bite, Headbutt, DragonBreath, Roar, Crunch, Slam, Dragon Pulse, Work Up, Dragon Rush, Body Slam, Scary Face, Hyper Voice, Outrage

POKÉMON BLACK VERSION: This brutal Pokémon travels the skies on its six wings. Anything that moves seems like a foe to it, triggering its attack.

POKÉMON WHITE VERSION: The heads on their arms do not have brains. They use all three heads to consume and destroy everything.

Deino → Level 50 → Zweilous → Level 64 → Hydreigon

EVOLUTIONS

41

JELLICENT
FLOATING POKÉMON

Jellicent ♂

Jellicent ♀

HOW TO SAY IT: JEL-ih-sent
POKÉDEX NUMBER: 099
TYPE: Water-Ghost
ABILITY: Water Absorb/Cursed Body
HEIGHT: 7' 03"
WEIGHT: 297.6 lbs.

POSSIBLE MOVES: Bubble, Water Sport, Absorb, Night Shade, BubbleBeam, Recover, Water Pulse, Ominous Wind, Brine, Rain Dance, Hex, Hydro Pump, Wring Out, Water Spout

Frillish → Level 40 → Jellicent

EVOLUTIONS

POKÉMON BLACK VERSION: The fate of the ships and crew that wander into Jellicent's habitat: all sunken, all lost, all vanished.

POKÉMON WHITE VERSION: They propel themselves by expelling absorbed seawater from their bodies. Their favorite food is life energy.

JOLTIK
ATTACHING POKÉMON

HOW TO SAY IT: JOHL-tik
POKÉDEX NUMBER: 101
TYPE: Bug-Electric
ABILITY: Compoundeyes/Unnerve
HEIGHT: 0' 04"
WEIGHT: 1.3 lbs.

POSSIBLE MOVES: String Shot, Leech Life, Spider Web, Thunder Wave, Screech, Fury Cutter, Electroweb, Bug Bite, Gastro Acid, Slash, Electro Ball, Signal Beam, Agility, Sucker Punch, Discharge, Bug Buzz

POKÉMON BLACK VERSION: Joltik that live in cities have learned a technique for sucking electricity from the outlets in houses.

POKÉMON WHITE VERSION: They attach themselves to large-bodied Pokémon and absorb static electricity, which they store in an electric pouch.

Joltik → Level 36 → Galvantula

EVOLUTIONS

KARRABLAST
CLAMPING POKÉMON

HOW TO SAY IT: KAIR-ruh-blast

POKÉDEX NUMBER: 094

TYPE: Bug

ABILITY: Swarm/Shed Skin

HEIGHT: 1' 08"

WEIGHT: 13.0 lbs.

POSSIBLE MOVES: Peck, Leer, Endure, Fury Cutter, Fury Attack, Headbutt, False Swipe, Bug Buzz, Slash, Take Down, Scary Face, X-Scissor, Flail, Swords Dance, Double-Edge

POKÉMON BLACK VERSION: These mysterious Pokémon evolve when they receive electrical stimulation while they are in the same place as Shelmet.

POKÉMON WHITE VERSION: When they feel threatened, they spit an acidic liquid to drive attackers away. This Pokémon targets Shelmet.

Karrablast

Link Trade Shelmet and Karrablast

Escavalier

EVOLUTIONS

KLANG
GEAR POKÉMON

HOW TO SAY IT: KLANG

POKÉDEX NUMBER: 106

TYPE: Steel

ABILITY: Plus/Minus

HEIGHT: 2' 00"

WEIGHT: 112.4 lbs.

POSSIBLE MOVES:
ViceGrip, Charge, ThunderShock, Gear Grind, Bind, Charge Beam, Autotomize, Mirror Shot, Screech, Discharge, Metal Sound, Shift Gear, Lock-On, Zap Cannon, Hyper Beam

POKÉMON BLACK VERSION:
By changing the direction in which it rotates, it communicates its feelings to others. When angry, it rotates faster.

POKÉMON WHITE VERSION:
Spinning minigears are rotated at high speed and repeatedly fired away. It is dangerous if the gears don't return.

Klink → Level 38 → Klang → Level 49 → Klinklang

EVOLUTIONS

KLINK
GEAR POKÉMON

HOW TO SAY IT: KLEENK
POKÉDEX NUMBER: 105
TYPE: Steel
ABILITY: Plus/Minus
HEIGHT: 1' 00"
WEIGHT: 46.3 lbs.

POSSIBLE MOVES: ViceGrip, Charge, ThunderShock, Gear Grind, Bind, Charge Beam, Autotomize, Mirror Shot, Screech, Discharge, Metal Sound, Shift Gear, Lock-On, Zap Cannon, Hyper Beam

Klink — Level 38 — Klang — Level 49 — Klinklang

EVOLUTIONS

POKÉMON BLACK VERSION: The two minigears that mesh together are predetermined. Each will rebound from other minigears without meshing.

POKÉMON WHITE VERSION: Interlocking two bodies and spinning around generates the energy they need to live.

KLINKLANG
GEAR POKÉMON

HOW TO SAY IT: KLEENK-klang
POKÉDEX NUMBER: 107
TYPE: Steel
ABILITY: Plus/Minus
HEIGHT: 2' 00"
WEIGHT: 178.6 lbs.

POSSIBLE MOVES: ViceGrip, Charge, ThunderShock, Gear Grind, Bind, Charge Beam, Autotomize, Mirror Shot, Screech, Discharge, Metal Sound, Shift Gear, Lock-On, Zap Cannon, Hyper Beam

Klink — Level 38 — Klang — Level 49 — Klinklang

EVOLUTIONS

POKÉMON BLACK VERSION: Its red core functions as an energy tank. It fires the charged energy through its spikes into an area.

POKÉMON WHITE VERSION: The gear with the red core is rotated at high speed for a rapid energy charge.

KROKOROK
DESERT CROC POKÉMON

HOW TO SAY IT: KRAHK-oh-rahk
POKÉDEX NUMBER: 058
TYPE: Ground-Dark
ABILITY: Intimidate/Moxie
HEIGHT: 3' 03"
WEIGHT: 73.6 lbs.

POSSIBLE MOVES: Leer, Rage, Bite, Sand-Attack, Torment, Sand Tomb, Assurance, Mud-Slap, Embargo, Swagger, Crunch, Dig, Scary Face, Foul Play, Sandstorm, Earthquake, Thrash

POKÉMON BLACK VERSION: They live in groups of a few individuals. Protective membranes shield their eyes from sandstorms.

POKÉMON WHITE VERSION: The special membrane covering its eyes can sense the heat of objects, so it can see its surroundings even in darkness.

Sandile → Level 29 → Krokorok → Level 40 → Krookodile
EVOLUTIONS

KROOKODILE
INTIMIDATION POKÉMON

HOW TO SAY IT: KROOK-oh-dyle
POKÉDEX NUMBER: 059
TYPE: Ground-Dark
ABILITY: Intimidate/Moxie
HEIGHT: 4' 11"
WEIGHT: 212.3 lbs.

POSSIBLE MOVES: Leer, Rage, Bite, Sand-Attack, Torment, Sand Tomb, Assurance, Mud-Slap, Embargo, Swagger, Crunch, Dig, Scary Face, Foul Play, Sandstorm, Earthquake, Outrage

POKÉMON BLACK VERSION: They never allow prey to escape. Their jaws are so powerful, they can crush the body of an automobile.

POKÉMON WHITE VERSION: It can expand the focus of its eyes, enabling it to see objects in the far distance as if it were using binoculars.

Sandile → Level 29 → Krokorok → Level 40 → Krookodile
EVOLUTIONS

KYUREM
BOUNDARY POKÉMON

HOW TO SAY IT: KYOO-rem
POKÉDEX NUMBER: 152
TYPE: Dragon-Ice
ABILITY: Pressure
HEIGHT: 9' 10"
WEIGHT: 716.5 lbs.

POSSIBLE MOVES: Icy Wind, Dragon Rage, Imprison, AncientPower, Ice Beam, DragonBreath, Slash, Scary Face, Glaciate, Dragon Pulse, Imprison, Endeavor, Blizzard, Outrage, Hyper Voice

POKÉMON BLACK VERSION:
It generates a powerful, freezing energy inside itself, but its body became frozen when the energy leaked out.

POKÉMON WHITE VERSION:
It can produce ultracold air. Its body is frozen.

DOES NOT EVOLVE

LAMPENT
LAMP POKÉMON

HOW TO SAY IT: LAM-pent
POKÉDEX NUMBER: 114
TYPE: Ghost-Fire
ABILITY: Flash Fire/Flame Body
HEIGHT: 2' 00"
WEIGHT: 28.7 lbs.
POSSIBLE MOVES: Ember, Astonish, Minimize, Smog, Fire Spin, Confuse Ray, Night Shade, Will-O-Wisp, Flame Burst, Imprison, Hex, Memento, Inferno, Curse, Shadow Ball, Pain Split, Overheat

POKÉMON BLACK VERSION: This ominous Pokémon is feared. Through cities it wanders, searching for the spirits of the fallen.

POKÉMON WHITE VERSION: It arrives near the moment of death and steals spirit from the body.

Litwick — Level 41 → Lampent — Dusk Stone → Chandelure

EVOLUTIONS

LANDORUS
ABUNDANCE POKÉMON

HOW TO SAY IT: LAN-duh-rus
POKÉDEX NUMBER: 151
TYPE: Ground-Flying
ABILITY: Sand Force
HEIGHT: 4' 11"
WEIGHT: 149.9 lbs.

POSSIBLE MOVES: Block, Mud Shot, Rock Tomb, Imprison, Punishment, Bulldoze, Rock Throw, Extrasensory, Swords Dance, Earth Power, Rock Slide, Earthquake, Sandstorm, Fissure, Stone Edge, Hammer Arm, Outrage

POKÉMON BLACK VERSION:
Lands visited by Landorus grant such bountiful crops that it has been hailed as "The Guardian of the Fields."

POKÉMON WHITE VERSION:
The energy that comes pouring from its tail increases the nutrition in the soil, making crops grow to great size.

DOES NOT EVOLVE

LARVESTA
TORCH POKÉMON

HOW TO SAY IT: lar-VESS-tah
POKÉDEX NUMBER: 142
TYPE: Bug-Fire
ABILITY: Flame Body
HEIGHT: 3' 07"
WEIGHT: 63.5 lbs.
POSSIBLE MOVES: Ember, String Shot, Leech Life, Take Down, Flame Charge, Bug Bite, Double-Edge, Flame Wheel, Bug Buzz, Amnesia, Thrash, Flare Blitz

POKÉMON BLACK VERSION:
This Pokémon was believed to have been born from the sun. When it evolves, its entire body is engulfed in flames.

POKÉMON WHITE VERSION:
The base of volcanoes is where they make their homes. They shoot fire from their five horns to repel attacking enemies.

Larvesta   Level 59   Volcarona
EVOLUTIONS

LEAVANNY
NURTURING POKÉMON

HOW TO SAY IT: lee-VAN-nee
POKÉDEX NUMBER: 48
TYPE: Bug-Grass
ABILITY: Swarm/Chlorophyll
HEIGHT: 3' 11"
WEIGHT: 45.2 lbs.

POSSIBLE MOVES: False Swipe, Tackle, String Shot, Bug Bite, Razor Leaf, Struggle Bug, Slash, Helping Hand, Leaf Blade, X-Scissor, Entrainment, Swords Dance, Leaf Storm

POKÉMON BLACK VERSION: It keeps its eggs warm with heat from fermenting leaves. It also uses leaves to make warm wrappings for Sewaddle.

POKÉMON WHITE VERSION: Upon finding a small Pokémon, it weaves clothing for it from leaves, using the cutters on its arms and sticky silk.

Sewaddle — Level 20 → Swadloon — Level up with high friendship → Leavanny

EVOLUTIONS

LIEPARD
CRUEL POKÉMON

HOW TO SAY IT: LY-purd
POKÉDEX NUMBER: 016
TYPE: Dark
ABILITY: Limber/Unburden
HEIGHT: 3' 07"
WEIGHT: 82.7 lbs.
POSSIBLE MOVES: Scratch, Growl, Assist, Sand-Attack, Fury Swipes, Pursuit, Torment, Fake Out, Hone Claws, Assurance, Slash, Taunt, Night Slash, Snatch, Nasty Plot, Sucker Punch

Purrloin → Level 20 → Liepard
EVOLUTIONS

POKÉMON BLACK VERSION: These Pokémon vanish and appear unexpectedly. Many Trainers are drawn to their beautiful form and fur.

POKÉMON WHITE VERSION: Stealthily, it sneaks up on its target, striking from behind before its victim has a chance to react.

LILLIGANT
FLOWERING POKÉMON

HOW TO SAY IT: LIL-lih-gunt
POKÉDEX NUMBER: 055
TYPE: Grass
ABILITY: Chlorophyll/Own Tempo
HEIGHT: 3' 07"
WEIGHT: 35.9 lbs.
POSSIBLE MOVES: Growth, Leech Seed, Mega Drain, Synthesis, Teeter Dance, Quiver Dance, Petal Dance

Petilil → Sun Stone → Lilligant
EVOLUTIONS

POKÉMON BLACK VERSION: Even veteran Trainers face a challenge in getting its beautiful flower to bloom. This Pokémon is popular with celebrities.

POKÉMON WHITE VERSION: The fragrance of the garland on its head has a relaxing effect. It withers if a Trainer does not take good care of it.

LILLIPUP
PUPPY POKÉMON

HOW TO SAY IT: LIL-ee-pup
POKÉDEX NUMBER: 012
TYPE: Normal
ABILITY: Vital Spirit/Pickup
HEIGHT: 1' 04"
WEIGHT: 9.0 lbs.
POSSIBLE MOVES: Leer, Tackle, Odor Sleuth, Bite, Helping Hand, Take Down, Work Up, Crunch, Roar, Retaliate, Reversal, Last Resort, Giga Impact

POKÉMON BLACK VERSION: It faces strong opponents with great courage. But, when at a disadvantage in a fight, this intelligent Pokémon flees.

POKÉMON WHITE VERSION: The long hair around its face provides an amazing radar that lets it sense subtle changes in its surroundings.

Lillipup → Level 16 → Herdier → Level 32 → Stoutland

EVOLUTIONS

LITWICK
CANDLE POKÉMON

HOW TO SAY IT: LIT-wik
POKÉDEX NUMBER: 113
TYPE: Ghost-Fire
ABILITY: Flash Fire/Flame Body
HEIGHT: 1' 00"
WEIGHT: 6.8 lbs.

POSSIBLE MOVES: Ember, Astonish, Minimize, Smog, Fire Spin, Confuse Ray, Night Shade, Will-O-Wisp, Flame Burst, Imprison, Hex, Memento, Inferno, Curse, Shadow Ball, Pain Split, Overheat

Litwick → Level 41 → Lampent → Dusk Stone → Chandelure

EVOLUTIONS

POKÉMON BLACK VERSION: Litwick shines a light that absorbs the life energy of people and Pokémon, which becomes the fuel that it burns.

POKÉMON WHITE VERSION: While shining a light and pretending to be a guide, it leeches off the life force of any who follow it.

MANDIBUZZ
BONE VULTURE POKÉMON

HOW TO SAY IT: MAN-dih-buz
POKÉDEX NUMBER: 136
TYPE: Dark-Flying
ABILITY: Big Pecks/Overcoat
HEIGHT: 3' 11"
WEIGHT: 87.1 lbs.

POSSIBLE MOVES: Gust, Leer, Fury Attack, Pluck, Nasty Plot, Flatter, Faint Attack, Punishment, Defog, Tailwind, Air Slash, Dark Pulse, Embargo, Bone Rush, Whirlwind, Brave Bird, Mirror Move

Vullaby → Level 54 → Mandibuzz

EVOLUTIONS

POKÉMON BLACK VERSION: It makes a nest out of bones it finds. It grabs weakened prey in its talons and hauls it to its nest of bones.

POKÉMON WHITE VERSION: Watching from the sky, they swoop to strike weakened Pokémon on the ground. They decorate themselves with bones

MARACTUS
CACTUS POKÉMON

HOW TO SAY IT: mah-RAK-tus

POKÉDEX NUMBER: 062

TYPE: Grass

ABILITY: Water Absorb/Chlorophyll

HEIGHT: 3' 03"

WEIGHT: 61.7 lbs.

POSSIBLE MOVES: Peck, Absorb, Sweet Scent, Growth, Pin Missile, Mega Drain, Synthesis, Cotton Spore, Needle Arm, Giga Drain, Acupressure, Ingrain, Petal Dance, Sucker Punch, Sunny Day, SolarBeam, Cotton Guard, After You

POKÉMON BLACK VERSION: It uses an up-tempo song and dance to drive away the bird Pokémon that prey on its flower seeds.

POKÉMON WHITE VERSION: Arid regions are their habitat. They move rhythmically, making a sound similar to maracas.

DOES NOT EVOLVE

MIENFOO
MARTIAL ARTS POKÉMON

HOW TO SAY IT: MEEN-FOO
POKÉDEX NUMBER: 125
TYPE: Fighting
ABILITY: Inner Focus/Regenerator
HEIGHT: 2' 11"
WEIGHT: 44.1 lbs.
POSSIBLE MOVES: Pound, Meditate, Detect,
Fake Out, DoubleSlap, Swift, Calm Mind,
Force Palm, Drain Punch, Jump Kick,
U-turn, Quick Guard, Bounce, Hi Jump Kick,
Reversal, Aura Sphere

Mienfoo → Level 50 → Mienshao
EVOLUTIONS

POKÉMON BLACK VERSION:
In fights, they dominate
with onslaughts of flowing,
continuous attacks. With their
sharp claws, they cut enemies.

POKÉMON WHITE VERSION:
They have mastered elegant
combos. As they concentrate,
their battle moves become
swifter and more precise.

MIENSHAO
MARTIAL ARTS POKÉMON

HOW TO SAY IT: MEEN-SHOW
POKÉDEX NUMBER: 126
TYPE: Fighting
ABILITY: Inner Focus/Regenerator
HEIGHT: 4' 07"
WEIGHT: 78.3 lbs.
POSSIBLE MOVES: Pound, Meditate, Detect,
Fake Out, DoubleSlap, Swift, Calm Mind,
Force Palm, Drain Punch, Jump Kick, U-turn,
Wide Guard, Bounce, Hi Jump Kick, Reversal,
Aura Sphere

Mienfoo → Level 50 → Mienshao
EVOLUTIONS

POKÉMON BLACK VERSION:
It wields the fur on its arms like
a whip. Its arm attacks come
with such rapidity that they
cannot even be seen.

POKÉMON WHITE VERSION:
They use the long fur on their
arms as a whip to strike their
opponents.

MINCCINO
CHINCHILLA POKÉMON

HOW TO SAY IT: min-CHEE-noh
POKÉDEX NUMBER: 078
TYPE: Normal
ABILITY: Cute Charm/Technician
HEIGHT: 1' 04"
WEIGHT: 12.8 lbs.
POSSIBLE MOVES: Pound, Growl, Helping Hand, Tickle, DoubleSlap, Encore, Swift, Sing, Tail Slap, Charm, Wake-Up Slap, Echoed Voice, Slam, Captivate, Hyper Voice, Last Resort, After You

POKÉMON BLACK VERSION: They greet one another by rubbing each other with their tails, which are always kept well groomed and clean.

POKÉMON WHITE VERSION: These Pokémon prefer a tidy habitat. They are always sweeping and dusting, using their tails as brooms.

Minccino → Shiny Stone → Cinccino

EVOLUTIONS

MUNNA
DREAM EATER POKÉMON

HOW TO SAY IT: MOON-nuh
POKÉDEX NUMBER: 023
TYPE: Psychic
ABILITY: Forewarn/Synchronize
HEIGHT: 2' 00"
WEIGHT: 51.4 lbs.

POSSIBLE MOVES: Psywave, Defense Curl, Lucky Chant, Yawn, Psybeam, Imprison, Moonlight, Hypnosis, Zen Headbutt, Synchronoise, Nightmare, Future Sight, Calm Mind, Psychic, Dream Eater, Telekinesis, Stored Power

Munna → Moon Stone → Musharna
EVOLUTIONS

POKÉMON BLACK VERSION:
Munna always float in the air. People whose dreams are eaten by them forget what the dreams had been about.

POKÉMON WHITE VERSION:
It eats the dreams of people and Pokémon. When it eats a pleasant dream, it expels pink colored mist.

MUSHARNA
DROWSING POKÉMON

HOW TO SAY IT: moo-SHAHR-nuh
POKÉDEX NUMBER: 024
TYPE: Psychic
ABILITY: Forewarn/Synchronize
HEIGHT: 3' 07"
WEIGHT: 133.4 lbs.

POSSIBLE MOVES: Defense Curl, Lucky Chant, Psybeam, Hypnosis

Munna → Moon Stone → Musharna
EVOLUTIONS

POKÉMON BLACK VERSION:
The mist emanating from their foreheads is packed with the dreams of people and Pokémon.

POKÉMON WHITE VERSION:
With the mist from its forehead, it can create shapes of things from dreams it has eaten.

OSHAWOTT
SEA OTTER POKÉMON

HOW TO SAY IT: AH-shah-wot
POKÉDEX NUMBER: 007
TYPE: Water
ABILITY: Torrent
HEIGHT: 1' 08"
WEIGHT: 13.0 lbs.

POSSIBLE MOVES: Tackle, Tail Whip, Water Gun, Water Sport, Focus Energy, Razor Shell, Fury Cutter, Water Pulse, Revenge, Aqua Jet, Encore, Aqua Tail, Retaliate, Swords Dance, Hydro Pump

POKÉMON BLACK VERSION:
It fights using the scalchop on its stomach. In response to an attack, it retaliates immediately by slashing.

POKÉMON WHITE VERSION:
The scalchop on its stomach is made from the same elements as claws. It detaches the scalchop for use as a blade.

What's a scalchop?
It's an item worn by Oshawott and Dewott. The scalchop is a hardened secretion made from a material similar to the enamel on teeth. Oshawott and Dewott can detach their scalchops and use them for battling; Oshawott also uses its scalchop for grooming.

Oshawott → Level 17 → Dewott → Level 36 → Samurott

EVOLUTIONS

PALPITOAD
VIBRATION POKÉMON

HOW TO SAY IT: PAL-pih-tohd
POKÉDEX NUMBER: 042
TYPE: Water-Ground
ABILITY: Swift Swim/Hydration
HEIGHT: 2' 07"
WEIGHT: 37.5 lbs.

POSSIBLE MOVES: Bubble, Growl, Supersonic, Round, BubbleBeam, Mud Shot, Aqua Ring, Uproar, Muddy Water, Rain Dance, Flail, Echoed Voice, Hydro Pump, Hyper Voice

POKÉMON BLACK VERSION: When they vibrate the bumps on their heads, they can make waves in water or earthquake-like vibrations on land.

POKÉMON WHITE VERSION: It lives in the water and on land. It uses its long, sticky tongue to capture prey.

Tympole → Level 25 → Palpitoad → Level 36 → Seismitoad

EVOLUTIONS

PANPOUR
SPRAY POKÉMON

HOW TO SAY IT: PAN-por
POKÉDEX NUMBER: 021
TYPE: Water
ABILITY: Gluttony
HEIGHT: 2' 00"
WEIGHT: 29.8 lbs.

POSSIBLE MOVES: Scratch, Leer, Lick, Water Gun, Fury Swipes, Water Sport, Bite, Scald, Taunt, Fling, Acrobatics, Brine, Recycle, Natural Gift, Crunch

POKÉMON BLACK VERSION: The water stored inside the tuft on its head is full of nutrients. Plants that receive its water grow large.

POKÉMON WHITE VERSION: It does not thrive in dry environments. It keeps itself damp by shooting water stored in its head tuft from its tail.

Panpour → **Water Stone** → Simipour

EVOLUTIONS

PANSAGE
GRASS MONKEY POKÉMON

HOW TO SAY IT: PAN-sayj
POKÉDEX NUMBER: 017
TYPE: Grass
ABILITY: Gluttony
HEIGHT: 2' 00"
WEIGHT: 23.1 lbs.

POSSIBLE MOVES: Scratch, Leer, Lick, Vine Whip, Fury Swipes, Leech Seed, Bite, Seed Bomb, Torment, Fling, Acrobatics, Grass Knot, Recycle, Natural Gift, Crunch

Pansage → Leaf Stone → Simisage
EVOLUTIONS

POKÉMON BLACK VERSION:
This Pokémon dwells deep in the forest. Eating a leaf from its head whisks weariness away as if by magic.

POKÉMON WHITE VERSION:
It shares the leaf on its head with weary-looking Pokémon. These leaves are known to relieve stress.

PANSEAR
HIGH TEMP POKÉMON

HOW TO SAY IT: PAN-seer
POKÉDEX NUMBER: 019
TYPE: Fire
ABILITY: Gluttony
HEIGHT: 2' 00"
WEIGHT: 24.3 lbs

POSSIBLE MOVES: Scratch, Leer, Lick, Incinerate, Fury Swipes, Yawn, Bite, Flame Burst, Amnesia, Fling, Acrobatics, Fire Blast, Recycle, Natural Gift, Crunch

Pansear → Fire Stone → Simisear
EVOLUTIONS

POKÉMON BLACK VERSION:
When it is angered, the temperature of its head tuft reaches 600° F. It uses its tuft to roast berries.

POKÉMON WHITE VERSION:
This Pokémon lives in caves in volcanoes. The fire within the tuft on its head can reach 600° F.

PATRAT
SCOUT POKÉMON

HOW TO SAY IT: pat-RAT

POKÉDEX NUMBER: 010

TYPE: Normal

ABILITY: Run Away/Keen Eye

HEIGHT: 1' 08"

WEIGHT: 25.6 lbs.

POSSIBLE MOVES: Tackle, Leer, Bite, Bide, Detect, Sand-Attack, Crunch, Hypnosis, Super Fang, After You, Work Up, Hyper Fang, Mean Look, Baton Pass, Slam

POKÉMON BLACK VERSION: Using food stored in cheek pouches, they can keep watch for days. They use their tails to communicate with others.

POKÉMON WHITE VERSION: Extremely cautious, they take shifts to maintain a constant watch of their nest. They feel insecure without a lookout.

Patrat   Level 20   Watchog

EVOLUTIONS

PAWNIARD
SHARP BLADE POKÉMON

HOW TO SAY IT: PAWN-yard
POKÉDEX NUMBER: 130
TYPE: Dark-Steel
ABILITY: Defiant/Inner Focus
HEIGHT: 1' 08"
WEIGHT: 22.5 lbs.
POSSIBLE MOVES: Scratch, Leer, Fury Cutter, Torment, Faint Attack, Scary Face, Metal Claw, Slash, Assurance, Metal Sound, Embargo, Iron Defense, Night Slash, Iron Head, Swords Dance, Guillotine

Pawniard — Level 52 — Bisharp

EVOLUTIONS

POKÉMON BLACK VERSION: Blades comprise this Pokémon's entire body. If battling dulls the blades, it sharpens them on stones by the river.

POKÉMON WHITE VERSION: They fight at Bisharp's command. They cling to their prey and inflict damage by sinking their blades into it.

PETILIL
BULB POKÉMON

HOW TO SAY IT: PEH-tuh-LIL
POKÉDEX NUMBER: 054
TYPE: Grass
ABILITY: Chlorophyll/Own Tempo
HEIGHT: 1' 08"
WEIGHT: 14.6 lbs.
POSSIBLE MOVES: Absorb, Growth, Leech Seed, Sleep Powder, Mega Drain, Synthesis, Magical Leaf, Stun Spore, Giga Drain, Aromatherapy, Helping Hand, Energy Ball, Entrainment, Sunny Day, After You, Leaf Storm

Petilil — Sun Stone — Lilligant

EVOLUTIONS

POKÉMON BLACK VERSION: The leaves on its head are very bitter. Eating one of these leaves is known to refresh a tired body.

POKÉMON WHITE VERSION: Since they prefer moist, nutrient-rich soil, the areas where Petilil live are known to be good for growing plants.

PIDOVE
TINY PIGEON POKÉMON

HOW TO SAY IT: pih-DUV

POKÉDEX NUMBER: 025

TYPE: Normal-Flying

ABILITY: Big Pecks/ Super Luck

HEIGHT: 1' 00"

WEIGHT: 4.6 lbs.

POSSIBLE MOVES: Gust, Growl, Leer, Quick Attack, Air Cutter, Roost, Detect, Taunt, Air Slash, Razor Wind, FeatherDance, Swagger, Facade, Tailwind, Sky Attack

POKÉMON BLACK VERSION: Each follows its Trainer's orders as best it can, but they sometimes fail to understand complicated commands.

POKÉMON WHITE VERSION: These Pokémon live in cities. They are accustomed to people. Flocks often gather in parks and plazas.

Pidove　　Level 21　　Tranquill　　Level 32　　Unfezant

EVOLUTIONS

PIGNITE
FIRE PIG POKÉMON

HOW TO SAY IT: pig-NYTE
POKÉDEX NUMBER: 005
TYPE: Fire-Fighting
ABILITY: Blaze
HEIGHT: 3' 03"
WEIGHT: 122.4 lbs.

POSSIBLE MOVES: Tackle, Tail Whip, Ember, Odor Sleuth, Defense Curl, Flame Charge, Arm Thrust, Smog, Rollout, Take Down, Heat Crash, Assurance, Flamethrower, Head Smash, Roar, Flare Blitz

Tepig → Level 17 → Pignite → Level 36 → Emboar
EVOLUTIONS

POKÉMON BLACK VERSION:
When its internal fire flares up, its movements grow sharper and faster. When in trouble, it emits smoke.

POKÉMON WHITE VERSION:
Whatever it eats becomes fuel for the flame in its stomach. When it is angered, the intensit of the flame increases.

PURRLOIN
DEVIOUS POKÉMON

HOW TO SAY IT: PUR-loyn
POKÉDEX NUMBER: 015
TYPE: Dark
ABILITY: Limber/Unburden
HEIGHT: 1' 04"
WEIGHT: 22.3 lbs.

POSSIBLE MOVES: Scratch, Growl, Assist, Sand-Attack, Fury Swipes, Pursuit, Torment, Fake Out, Hone Claws, Assurance, Slash, Captivate, Night Slash, Snatch, Nasty Plot, Sucker Punch

Purrloin → Level 20 → Liepard
EVOLUTIONS

POKÉMON BLACK VERSION:
They steal from people for fun, but their victims can't help but forgive them. Their deceptively cute act is perfect.

POKÉMON WHITE VERSION:
Its cute act is a ruse. When victims let down their guard, they find their items taken. It attacks with sharp claws.

RESHIRAM
VAST WHITE POKÉMON

HOW TO SAY IT: RESH-i-ram

POKÉDEX NUMBER: 149

TYPE: Dragon-Fire

ABILITY: Turboblaze

HEIGHT: 10' 06"

WEIGHT: 727.5 lbs.

POSSIBLE MOVES: Fire Fang, Dragon Rage, Imprison, AncientPower, Flamethrower, DragonBreath, Slash, Extrasensory, Fusion Flare, Dragon Pulse, Imprison, Crunch, Fire Blast, Outrage, Hyper Voice, Blue Flare

POKÉMON BLACK VERSION: This Pokémon appears in legends. It sends flames into the air from its tail, burning up everything around it.

POKÉMON WHITE VERSION: When Reshiram's tail flares, the heat energy moves the atmosphere and changes the world's weather.

DOES NOT EVOLVE

REUNICLUS
MULTIPLYING POKÉMON

HOW TO SAY IT: ree-yoo-NIH-klus
POKÉDEX NUMBER: 085
TYPE: Psychic
ABILITY: Overcoat/Magic Guard
HEIGHT: 3' 03"
WEIGHT: 44.3 lbs.
POSSIBLE MOVES: Psywave, Reflect, Rollout, Snatch, Hidden Power, Light Screen, Charm, Recover, Psyshock, Endeavor, Future Sight, Pain Split, Psychic, Dizzy Punch, Skill Swap, Heal Block, Wonder Room

POKÉMON BLACK VERSION: When Reuniclus shake hands, a network forms between their brains, increasing their psychic power.

POKÉMON WHITE VERSION: These remarkably intelligent Pokémon fight by controlling arms that can grip with rock-crushing power.

Solosis → Level 32 → Duosion → Level 41 → Reuniclus

EVOLUTIONS

ROGGENROLA
MANTLE POKÉMON

HOW TO SAY IT: rah-gen-ROH-lah
POKÉDEX NUMBER: 030
TYPE: Rock
ABILITY: Sturdy
HEIGHT: 1' 04"
WEIGHT: 39.7 lbs.
POSSIBLE MOVES: Tackle; Harden, Sand-Attack, Headbutt, Rock Blast, Mud-Slap, Iron Defense, Smack Down, Rock Slide, Stealth Rock, Sandstorm, Stone Edge, Explosion

POKÉMON BLACK VERSION: Its ear is hexagonal in shape. Compressed underground, its body is as hard as steel.

POKÉMON WHITE VERSION: They were discovered a hundred years ago in an earthquake fissure. Inside each one is an energy core.

Roggenrola → Level 25 → Boldore → Link Trade → Gigalith

EVOLUTIONS

RUFFLET
EAGLET POKÉMON

HOW TO SAY IT: RUF-lit
POKÉDEX NUMBER: 133
TYPE: Normal-Flying
ABILITY: Keen Eye/Sheer Force
HEIGHT: 1' 08"
WEIGHT: 23.1 lbs.
POSSIBLE MOVES: Peck, Leer, Fury Attack, Wing Attack, Hone Claws, Scary Face, Aerial Ace, Slash, Defog, Tailwind, Air Slash, Crush Claw, Sky Drop, Whirlwind, Brave Bird, Thrash

POKÉMON BLACK VERSION: They crush berries with their talons. They bravely stand up to any opponent, no matter how strong it is.

POKÉMON WHITE VERSION: They will challenge anything, even strong opponents, without fear. Their frequent fights help them become stronger.

Rufflet → Level 54 → Braviary

EVOLUTIONS

SAMUROTT
FORMIDABLE POKÉMON

HOW TO SAY IT: SAM-oo-rot
POKÉDEX NUMBER: 009
TYPE: Water
ABILITY: Torrent
HEIGHT: 4' 11"
WEIGHT: 208.6 lbs.
POSSIBLE MOVES: Megahorn, Tackle, Tail Whip, Water Gun, Water Sport, Focus Energy, Razor Shell, Fury Cutter, Water Pulse, Revenge, Aqua Jet, Slash, Encore, Aqua Tail, Retaliate, Swords Dance, Hydro Pump

POKÉMON BLACK VERSION:
One swing of the sword incorporated in its armor can fell an opponent. A simple glare from one of them quiets everybody.

POKÉMON WHITE VERSION:
Part of the armor on its anterior legs becomes a giant sword. Its cry alone is enough to intimidate most enemies.

Oshawott → Level 17 → Dewott → Level 36 → Samurott

EVOLUTIONS

SANDILE
DESERT CROC POKÉMON

HOW TO SAY IT: SAN-dyle
POKÉDEX NUMBER: 057
TYPE: Ground-Dark
ABILITY: Intimidate/Moxie
HEIGHT: 2' 04"
WEIGHT: 33.5 lbs.
POSSIBLE MOVES: Leer, Rage, Bite, Sand-Attack, Torment, Sand Tomb, Assurance, Mud-Slap, Embargo, Swagger, Crunch, Dig, Scary Face, Foul Play, Sandstorm, Earthquake, Thrash

POKÉMON BLACK VERSION: They live buried in the sands of the desert. The sun-warmed sands prevent their body temperature from dropping.

POKÉMON WHITE VERSION: It moves along below the sand's surface, except for its nose and eyes. A dark membrane shields its eyes from the sun.

Level 29 Level 40

Sandile   Krokorok   Krookodile

EVOLUTIONS

SAWK
KARATE POKÉMON

HOW TO SAY IT: SAWK
POKÉDEX NUMBER: 045
TYPE: Fighting
ABILITY: Sturdy/Inner Focus
HEIGHT: 4' 07"
WEIGHT: 112.4 lbs.
POSSIBLE MOVES: Rock Smash, Leer, Bide, Focus Energy, Double Kick, Low Sweep, Counter, Karate Chop, Brick Break, Bulk Up, Retaliate, Endure, Quick Guard, Close Combat, Reversal

POKÉMON BLACK VERSION: The sound of Sawk punching boulders and trees can be heard all the way from the mountains where they train.

POKÉMON WHITE VERSION: Tying their belts gets them pumped and makes their punches more destructive. Disturbing their training angers them.

DOES NOT EVOLVE

SAWSBUCK
SEASON POKÉMON

HOW TO SAY IT: SAWZ-buk

POKÉDEX NUMBER: 092

TYPE: Normal-Grass

ABILITY: Chlorophyll/Sap Sipper

HEIGHT: 6' 03"

WEIGHT: 203.9 lbs.

POSSIBLE MOVES: Megahorn, Tackle, Camouflage, Growl, Sand-Attack, Double Kick, Leech Seed, Faint Attack, Take Down, Jump Kick, Aromatherapy, Energy Ball, Charm, Horn Leech, Nature Power, Double-Edge, SolarBeam

Spring Form

Summer Form

Autumn Form

Winter Form

POKÉMON BLACK VERSION: They migrate according to the seasons. People can tell the season by looking at Sawsbuck's horns.

POKÉMON WHITE VERSION: The plants growing on its horns change according to the season. The leaders of the herd possess magnificent horns.

Deerling

Level 34

Sawsbuck

EVOLUTIONS

SCOLIPEDE
MEGAPEDE POKÉMON

HOW TO SAY IT: SKOH-lih-peed

POKÉDEX NUMBER: 051

TYPE: Bug-Poison

ABILITY: Poison Point/Swarm

HEIGHT: 8' 02"

WEIGHT: 442.0 lbs.

POSSIBLE MOVES:
Megahorn, Defense Curl, Rollout, Poison Sting, Screech, Pursuit, Protect, Poison Tail, Bug Bite, Venoshock, Baton Pass, Agility, Steamroller, Toxic, Rock Climb, Double-Edge

POKÉMON BLACK VERSION: With quick movements, it chases down its foes, attacking relentlessly with its horns until it prevails.

POKÉMON WHITE VERSION: Highly aggressive, it uses the claws near its neck to dig into its opponents and poison them.

Venipede → Level 22 → Whirlipede → Level 30 → Scolipede

EVOLUTIONS

SCRAFTY
HOODLUM POKÉMON

HOW TO SAY IT: SKRAF-tee
POKÉDEX NUMBER: 066
TYPE: Dark-Fighting
ABILITY: Shed Skin/Moxie
HEIGHT: 3' 07"
WEIGHT: 66.1 lbs.

POSSIBLE MOVES: Leer, Low Kick, Sand-Attack, Faint Attack, Headbutt, Swagger, Brick Break, Payback, Chip Away, Hi Jump Kick, Scary Face, Crunch, Facade, Rock Climb, Focus Punch, Head Smash

Scraggy Level 39 Scrafty
EVOLUTIONS

POKÉMON BLACK VERSION: Groups of them beat up anything that enters their territory. Each can spit acidic liquid from its mouth.

POKÉMON WHITE VERSION: It can smash concrete blocks with its kicking attacks. The one with the biggest crest is the group leader.

SCRAGGY
SHEDDING POKÉMON

HOW TO SAY IT: SKRAG-ee
POKÉDEX NUMBER: 065
TYPE: Dark-Fighting
ABILITY: Shed Skin/Moxie
HEIGHT: 2' 00"
WEIGHT: 26.0 lbs.

POSSIBLE MOVES: Leer, Low Kick, Sand-Attack, Faint Attack, Headbutt, Swagger, Brick Break, Payback, Chip Away, Hi Jump Kick, Scary Face, Crunch, Facade, Rock Climb, Focus Punch, Head Smash

Scraggy Level 39 Scrafty
EVOLUTIONS

POKÉMON BLACK VERSION: Its skin has a rubbery elasticity, so it can reduce damage by defensively pulling its skin up to its neck.

POKÉMON WHITE VERSION: It immediately headbutts anyone that makes eye contact with it. Its skull is massively thick.

SEISMITOAD
VIBRATION POKÉMON

HOW TO SAY IT: SYZ-mih-tohd
POKÉDEX NUMBER: 043
TYPE: Water-Ground
ABILITY: Swift Swim/Poison Touch
HEIGHT: 4' 11"
WEIGHT: 136.7 lbs.

POSSIBLE MOVES: Bubble, Growl, Supersonic, Round, BubbleBeam, Mud Shot, Aqua Ring, Uproar, Muddy Water, Rain Dance, Acid, Flail, Drain Punch, Echoed Voice, Hydro Pump, Hyper Voice

POKÉMON BLACK VERSION: They shoot paralyzing liquid from their head bumps. They use vibration to hurt their opponents.

POKÉMON WHITE VERSION: It increases the power of its punches by vibrating the bumps on its fists. It can turn a boulder to rubble with one punch.

Tympole → Level 25 → Palpitoad → Level 36 → Seismitoad

EVOLUTIONS

75

SERPERIOR
REGAL POKÉMON

HOW TO SAY IT: sur-PEER-ee-ur
POKÉDEX NUMBER: 003
TYPE: Grass
ABILITY: Overgrow
HEIGHT: 10' 10"
WEIGHT: 138.9 lbs.
POSSIBLE MOVES: Tackle, Leer, Vine Whip, Wrap, Growth, Leaf Tornado, Leech Seed, Mega Drain, Slam, Leaf Blade, Coil, Giga Drain, Wring Out, Gastro Acid, Leaf Storm

Snivy — Level 17 — Servine — Level 36 — Serperior

EVOLUTIONS

POKÉMON BLACK VERSION: It can stop its opponents' movements with just a glare. It takes in solar energy and boosts it internally.

POKÉMON WHITE VERSION: They raise their heads to intimidate opponents but only give it their all when fighting a powerful opponent.

SERVINE
GRASS SNAKE POKÉMON

HOW TO SAY IT: SUR-vine
POKÉDEX NUMBER: 002
TYPE: Grass
ABILITY: Overgrow
HEIGHT: 2' 07"
WEIGHT: 35.3 lbs.
POSSIBLE MOVES: Tackle, Leer, Vine Whip, Wrap, Growth, Leaf Tornado, Leech Seed, Mega Drain, Slam, Leaf Blade, Coil, Giga Drain, Wring Out, Gastro Acid, Leaf Storm

POKÉMON BLACK VERSION: It moves along the ground as if sliding. Its swift movements befuddle its foes, and it then attacks with a vine whip.

POKÉMON WHITE VERSION: They avoid attacks by sinking into the shadows of thick foliage. They retaliate with masterful whipping technique

Snivy — Level 17 — Servine — Level 36 — Serperior

EVOLUTIONS

SEWADDLE
SEWING POKÉMON

HOW TO SAY IT: seh-WAH-dul
POKÉDEX NUMBER: 046
TYPE: Bug-Grass
ABILITY: Swarm/Chlorophyll
HEIGHT: 1' 00"
WEIGHT: 5.5 lbs.
POSSIBLE MOVES: Tackle, String Shot, Bug Bite, Razor Leaf, Struggle Bug, Endure, Bug Buzz, Flail

POKÉMON BLACK VERSION:
Leavanny dress it in clothes they made for it when it hatched. It hides its head in its hood while it is sleeping.

POKÉMON WHITE VERSION:
This Pokémon makes clothes for itself. It chews up leaves and sews them with sticky thread extruded from its mouth.

Sewaddle → Level 20 → Swadloon → Level up with high friendship → Leavanny

EVOLUTIONS

SHELMET
SNAIL POKÉMON

HOW TO SAY IT: SHELL-meht
POKÉDEX NUMBER: 122
TYPE: Bug
ABILITY: Hydration/Shell Armor
HEIGHT: 1' 04"
WEIGHT: 17.0 lbs.
POSSIBLE MOVES: Leech Life, Acid, Bide, Curse, Struggle Bug, Mega Drain, Yawn, Protect, Acid Armor, Giga Drain, Body Slam, Bug Buzz, Recover, Guard Swap, Final Gambit

POKÉMON BLACK VERSION:
When attacked, it defends itself by closing the lid of its shell. It can spit a sticky, poisonous liquid.

POKÉMON WHITE VERSION:
It evolves when bathed in an electric-like energy along with Karrablast. The reason is still unknown.

Link Trade Karrablast and Shelmet

Shelmet → Accelgor

EVOLUTIONS

SIGILYPH
AVIANOID POKÉMON

HOW TO SAY IT: SIH-jih-liff
POKÉDEX NUMBER: 067
TYPE: Psychic-Flying
ABILITY: Marvel Skin/Magic Guard
HEIGHT: 4' 07"
WEIGHT: 30.9 lbs.
POSSIBLE MOVES: Gust, Miracle Eye, Hypnosis, Psywave, Tailwind, Whirlwind, Psybeam, Air Cutter, Light Screen, Reflect, Synchronoise, Mirror Move, Gravity, Air Slash, Psychic, Cosmic Power, Sky Attack

DOES NOT EVOLVE

POKÉMON BLACK VERSION:
They never vary the route they fly, because their memories of guarding an ancient city remain steadfast.

POKÉMON WHITE VERSION:
The guardians of an ancient city, they use their psychic power to attack enemies that invade their territory.

SIMIPOUR
GEYSER POKÉMON

HOW TO SAY IT: SIH-mee-por
POKÉDEX NUMBER: 022
TYPE: Water
ABILITY: Gluttony
HEIGHT: 3' 03"
WEIGHT: 63.9 lbs.
POSSIBLE MOVES: Leer, Lick, Fury Swipes, Scald

Panpour → Water Stone → Simipour

EVOLUTIONS

POKÉMON BLACK VERSION:
The tuft on its head holds water. When the level runs low, it replenishes the tuft by siphoning up water with its tail.

POKÉMON WHITE VERSION:
The high-pressure water expelled from its tail is so powerful, it can destroy a concrete wall.

SIMISAGE
THORN MONKEY POKÉMON

HOW TO SAY IT: SIH-mee-sayj
POKÉDEX NUMBER: 018
TYPE: Grass
ABILITY: Gluttony
HEIGHT: 3' 07"
WEIGHT: 67.2 lbs.
POSSIBLE MOVES: Leer, Lick, Fury Swipes, Seed Bomb

Pansage → **Leaf Stone** → Simisage

EVOLUTIONS

POKÉMON BLACK VERSION: Ill tempered, it fights by swinging its barbed tail around wildly. The leaf growing on its head is very bitter.

POKÉMON WHITE VERSION: It attacks enemies with strikes of its thorn-covered tail. This Pokémon is wild tempered.

SIMISEAR
EMBER POKÉMON

HOW TO SAY IT: SIH-mee-seer
POKÉDEX NUMBER: 020
TYPE: Fire
ABILITY: Gluttony
HEIGHT: 3' 03"
WEIGHT: 61.7 lbs.
POSSIBLE MOVES: Leer, Lick, Fury Swipes, Flame Burst

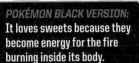

Pansear → **Fire Stone** → Simisear

EVOLUTIONS

POKÉMON BLACK VERSION: It loves sweets because they become energy for the fire burning inside its body.

POKÉMON WHITE VERSION: A flame burns inside its body. It scatters embers from its head and tail to sear its opponents.

SNIVY
GRASS SNAKE POKÉMON

HOW TO SAY IT: SNY-vee
POKÉDEX NUMBER: 001
TYPE: Grass
ABILITY: Overgrow
HEIGHT: 2' 00"
WEIGHT: 17.9 lbs.

POSSIBLE MOVES: Tackle, Leer, Vine Whip, Wrap, Growth, Leaf Tornado, Leech Seed, Mega Drain, Slam, Leaf Blade, Coil, Giga Drain, Wring Out, Gastro Acid, Leaf Storm

POKÉMON BLACK VERSION: It is very intelligent and calm. Being exposed to lots of sunlight makes its movements swifter.

POKÉMON WHITE VERSION: They photosynthesize by bathing their tails in sunlight. When they are not feeling well, their tails droop.

Snivy → Level 17 → Servine → Level 36 → Serperior

EVOLUTIONS

SOLOSIS
CELL POKÉMON

HOW TO SAY IT: soh-LOH-sis
POKÉDEX NUMBER: 083
TYPE: Psychic
ABILITY: Overcoat/Magic Guard
HEIGHT: 1' 00"
WEIGHT: 2.2 lbs.
POSSIBLE MOVES: Psywave, Reflect, Rollout, Snatch, Hidden Power, Light Screen, Charm, Recover, Psyshock, Endeavor, Future Sight, Pain Split, Psychic, Skill Swap, Heal Block, Wonder Room

POKÉMON BLACK VERSION: They drive away attackers by unleashing psychic power. They can use telepathy to talk with others.

POKÉMON WHITE VERSION: Because their bodies are enveloped in a special liquid, they can survive in any environment.

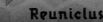

Solosis   Level 32   Duosion   Level 41   Reuniclus

EVOLUTIONS

STOUTLAND
BIG-HEARTED POKÉMON

HOW TO SAY IT: STOWT-lund
POKÉDEX NUMBER: 014
TYPE: Normal
ABILITY: Intimidate/Sand Rush
HEIGHT: 3' 11"
WEIGHT: 134.5 lbs.

POSSIBLE MOVES: Ice Fang, Fire Fang, Thunder Fang, Leer, Tackle, Odor Sleuth, Bite, Helping Hand, Take Down, Work Up, Crunch, Roar, Retaliate, Reversal, Last Resort, Giga Impact

Lillipup → Level 16 → Herdier → Level 32 → Stoutland
EVOLUTIONS

POKÉMON BLACK VERSION: It rescues people stranded by blizzards in the mountains. Its shaggy fur shields it from the cold.

POKÉMON WHITE VERSION: This extremely wise Pokémon excels at rescuing people stranded at sea or in the mountains.

STUNFISK
TRAP POKÉMON

HOW TO SAY IT: STUN-fisk
POKÉDEX NUMBER: 124
TYPE: Ground-Electric
ABILITY: Static/Limber
HEIGHT: 2' 04"
WEIGHT: 24.3 lbs.

POSSIBLE MOVES: Mud-Slap, Mud Sport, Bide, ThunderShock, Mud Shot, Camouflage, Mud Bomb, Discharge, Endure, Bounce, Muddy Water, Thunderbolt, Revenge, Flail, Fissure

POKÉMON BLACK VERSION: Its skin is very hard, so it is unhurt even if stepped on by sumo wrestlers. It smiles when transmitting electricity.

POKÉMON WHITE VERSION: It conceals itself in the mud of the seashore. Then it waits. When prey touch it, it delivers a jolt of electricity.

DOES NOT EVOLVE

SWADLOON
LEAF-WRAPPED POKÉMON

HOW TO SAY IT: SWAHD-loon
POKÉDEX NUMBER: 047
TYPE: Bug-Grass
ABILITY: Leaf Guard/Chlorophyll
HEIGHT: 1' 08"
WEIGHT: 16.1 lbs.
POSSIBLE MOVES: GrassWhistle, Tackle, String Shot, Bug Bite, Razor Leaf, Protect

POKÉMON BLACK VERSION: Forests where Swadloon live have superb foliage because the nutrients they make from fallen leaves nourish the plant life.

POKÉMON WHITE VERSION: It protects itself from the cold by wrapping up in leaves. It stays on the move, eating leaves in forests.

Sewaddle → Level 20 → Swadloon → Level up with high friendship → Leavanny

EVOLUTIONS

SWANNA
WHITE BIRD POKÉMON

HOW TO SAY IT: SWAH-nuh
POKÉDEX NUMBER: 087
TYPE: Water-Flying
ABILITY: Keen Eye/Big Pecks
HEIGHT: 4' 03"
WEIGHT: 53.4 lbs.
POSSIBLE MOVES:
Water Gun, Water Sport, Defog,
Wing Attack, Water Pulse, Aerial Ace, BubbleBeam,
FeatherDance, Aqua Ring, Air Slash,
Roost, Rain Dance, Tailwind,
Brave Bird, Hurricane

POKÉMON BLACK VERSION:
Swanna start to dance at dusk.
The one dancing in the middle is
the leader of the flock.

POKÉMON WHITE VERSION:
It administers sharp, powerful
pecks with its bill. It whips its
long neck to deliver forceful
repeated strikes.

Ducklett → Level 35 → Swanna

EVOLUTIONS

SWOOBAT
COURTING POKÉMON

HOW TO SAY IT: SWOO-bat
POKÉDEX NUMBER: 034
TYPE: Psychic-Flying
ABILITY: Unaware/Klutz
HEIGHT: 2' 11"
WEIGHT: 23.1 lbs.
POSSIBLE MOVES:
Confusion, Odor Sleuth, Gust, Assurance, Heart Stamp, Imprison, Air Cutter, Attract, Amnesia, Calm Mind, Air Slash, Future Sight, Psychic, Endeavor

POKÉMON BLACK VERSION:
It emits sound waves of various frequencies from its nose, including some powerful enough to destroy rocks.

POKÉMON WHITE VERSION:
Anyone who comes into contact with the ultrasonic waves emitted by a courting male experiences a positive mood shift.

Level up with high friendship

Woobat   Swoobat
EVOLUTIONS

TEPIG
FIRE PIG POKÉMON

HOW TO SAY IT: TEH-pig

POKÉDEX NUMBER: 004

TYPE: Fire

ABILITY: Blaze

HEIGHT: 1' 08"

WEIGHT: 21.8 lbs.

POSSIBLE MOVES: Tackle, Tail Whip, Ember, Odor Sleuth, Defense Curl, Flame Charge, Smog, Rollout, Take Down, Heat Crash, Assurance, Flamethrower, Head Smash, Roar, Flare Blitz

POKÉMON BLACK VERSION:
It can deftly dodge its foe's attacks while shooting fireballs from its nose. It roasts berries before it eats them.

POKÉMON WHITE VERSION:
It blows fire through its nose. When it catches a cold, the fire becomes pitch-black smoke instead.

Tepig → Level 17 → Pignite → Level 36 → Emboar

EVOLUTIONS

TERRAKION
CAVERN POKÉMON

HOW TO SAY IT: tur-RAK-ee-un
POKÉDEX NUMBER: 145
TYPE: Rock-Fighting
ABILITY: Justified
HEIGHT: 6' 03"
WEIGHT: 573.2 lbs.
POSSIBLE MOVES: Quick Attack, Leer, Double Kick, Smack Down, Take Down, Helping Hand, Retaliate, Rock Slide, Sacred Sword, Swords Dance, Quick Guard, Work Up, Stone Edge, Close Combat

LEGENDARY POKÉMON

POKÉMON BLACK VERSION: This Pokémon came to the defense of Pokémon that had lost their homes in a war among humans.

POKÉMON WHITE VERSION: Its charge is strong enough to break through a giant castle wall in one blow. This Pokémon is spoken of in legends.

DOES NOT EVOLVE

THROH
JUDO POKÉMON

HOW TO SAY IT: THROH

POKÉDEX NUMBER: 044

TYPE: Fighting

ABILITY: Guts/Inner Focus

HEIGHT: 4' 03"

WEIGHT: 122.4 lbs.

POSSIBLE MOVES: Bind, Leer, Bide, Focus Energy, Seismic Toss, Vital Throw, Revenge, Storm Throw, Body Slam, Bulk Up, Circle Throw, Endure, Wide Guard, Superpower, Reversal

POKÉMON BLACK VERSION: When it tightens its belt, it becomes stronger. Wild Throh use vines to weave their own belts.

POKÉMON WHITE VERSION: When they encounter foes bigger than themselves, they try to throw them. They always travel in packs of five.

DOES NOT EVOLVE

THUNDURUS
BOLT STRIKE POKÉMON

HOW TO SAY IT: THUN-duh-rus
POKÉDEX NUMBER: 148
TYPE: Electric-Flying
ABILITY: Prankster
HEIGHT: 4' 11"
WEIGHT: 134.5 lbs.
POSSIBLE MOVES: Uproar, Astonish, ThunderShock, Swagger, Bite, Revenge, Shock Wave, Heal Block, Agility, Discharge, Crunch, Charge, Nasty Plot, Thunder, Dark Pulse, Hammer Arm, Thrash

POKÉMON BLACK VERSION:
Countless charred remains mar the landscape of places through which Thundurus has passed.

POKÉMON WHITE VERSION:
The spikes on its tail discharge immense bolts of lightning. It flies around the Unova region firing off lightning bolts.

DOES NOT EVOLVE

TIMBURR
MUSCULAR POKÉMON

HOW TO SAY IT: TIM-bur
POKÉDEX NUMBER: 038
TYPE: Fighting
ABILITY: Guts/Sheer Force
HEIGHT: 2' 00"
WEIGHT: 27.6 lbs.
POSSIBLE MOVES: Pound, Leer, Focus Energy, Bide, Low Kick, Rock Throw, Wake-Up Slap, Chip Away, Bulk Up, Rock Slide, DynamicPunch, Scary Face, Hammer Arm, Stone Edge, Focus Punch, Superpower

POKÉMON BLACK VERSION: It fights by swinging a piece of lumber around. It is close to evolving when it can handle the lumber without difficulty.

POKÉMON WHITE VERSION: These Pokémon appear at building sites and help out with construction. They always carry squared logs.

Timburr → Level 25 → Gurdurr → Link Trade → Conkeldurr
EVOLUTIONS

TIRTOUGA
PROTOTURTLE POKÉMON

HOW TO SAY IT: teer-TOO-gah
POKÉDEX NUMBER: 070
TYPE: Water-Rock
ABILITY: Solid Rock/Sturdy
HEIGHT: 2' 04"
WEIGHT: 36.4 lbs.
POSSIBLE MOVES: Bide, Withdraw, Water Gun, Rollout, Bite, Protect, Aqua Jet, AncientPower, Crunch, Wide Guard, Brine, Smack Down, Curse, Shell Smash, Aqua Tail, Rock Slide, Rain Dance, Hydro Pump

POKÉMON BLACK VERSION: Restored from a fossil, this Pokémon can dive to depths beyond half a mile.

POKÉMON WHITE VERSION: About 100 million years ago, these Pokémon swam in oceans. It is thought they also went on land to attack prey.

Tirtouga → Level 37 → Carracosta
EVOLUTIONS

TORNADUS
CYCLONE POKÉMON

HOW TO SAY IT: tohr-NAY-dus
POKÉDEX NUMBER: 147
TYPE: Flying
ABILITY: Prankster
HEIGHT: 4' 11"
WEIGHT: 138.9 lbs.
POSSIBLE MOVES: Uproar, Astonish, Gust, Swagger, Bite, Revenge, Air Cutter, Extrasensory, Agility, Air Slash, Crunch, Tailwind, Rain Dance, Hurricane, Dark Pulse, Hammer Arm, Thrash

POKÉMON BLACK VERSION: The lower half of its body is wrapped in a cloud of energy. It zooms through the sky at 200 mph.

POKÉMON WHITE VERSION: Tornadus expels massive energy from its tail, causing severe storms. Its power is great enough to blow houses away.

DOES NOT EVOLVE

TRANQUILL

WILD PIGEON POKÉMON

HOW TO SAY IT: TRAN-kwil
POKÉDEX NUMBER: 026
TYPE: Normal-Flying
ABILITY: Big Pecks/Super Luck
HEIGHT: 2' 00"
WEIGHT: 33.1 lbs.
POSSIBLE MOVES: Gust, Growl, Leer, Quick Attack, Air Cutter, Roost, Detect, Taunt, Air Slash, Razor Wind, FeatherDance, Swagger, Facade, Tailwind, Sky Attack

Pidove → Level 21 → Tranquill → Level 32 → Unfezant

EVOLUTIONS

POKÉMON BLACK VERSION: It can return to its Trainer's location regardless of the distance separating them.

POKÉMON WHITE VERSION: Many people believe that, deep in the forest where Tranquill live, there is a peaceful place where there is no war.

TRUBBISH

TRASH BAG POKÉMON

HOW TO SAY IT: TRUB-bish
POKÉDEX NUMBER: 074
TYPE: Poison
ABILITY: Stench/Sticky Hold
HEIGHT: 2' 00"
WEIGHT: 68.3 lbs.
POSSIBLE MOVES: Pound, Poison Gas, Recycle, Toxic Spikes, Acid Spray, DoubleSlap, Sludge, Stockpile, Swallow, Take Down, Sludge Bomb, Clear Smog, Toxic, Amnesia, Gunk Shot, Explosion

Trubbish → Level 36 → Garbodor

EVOLUTIONS

POKÉMON BLACK VERSION: Inhaling the gas they belch will make you sleep for a week. They prefer unsanitary places.

POKÉMON WHITE VERSION: The combination of garbage bags and industrial waste caused the chemical reaction that created this Pokémon.

TYMPOLE
TADPOLE POKÉMON

HOW TO SAY IT: TIM-pohl
POKÉDEX NUMBER: 041
TYPE: Water
ABILITY: Swift Swim/Hydration
HEIGHT: 1' 08"
WEIGHT: 9.9 lbs.
POSSIBLE MOVES:
Bubble, Growl,
Supersonic, Round,
BubbleBeam, Mud Shot,
Aqua Ring, Uproar,
Muddy Water, Rain
Dance, Flail, Echoed Voice,
Hydro Pump, Hyper Voice

POKÉMON BLACK VERSION:
They warn others of danger
by vibrating their cheeks to
create a high-pitched sound.

POKÉMON WHITE VERSION:
By vibrating its cheeks, it emits
sound waves imperceptible to
humans. It uses the rhythm of
these sounds to talk.

Tympole → Level 25 → Palpitoad → Level 36 → Seismitoad

EVOLUTIONS

TYNAMO
ELEFISH POKÉMON

HOW TO SAY IT: TIE-nah-moh
POKÉDEX NUMBER: 108
TYPE: Electric
ABILITY: Levitate
HEIGHT: 0' 08"
WEIGHT: 0.7 lbs.
POSSIBLE MOVES: Tackle, Thunder
Wave, Spark, Charge Beam

POKÉMON BLACK VERSION:
While one alone doesn't have much power, a chain of many Tynamo can be as powerful as lightning.

POKÉMON WHITE VERSION:
These Pokémon move in schools. They have an electricity-generating organ, so they discharge electricity if in danger.

Tynamo → Level 39 → Eelektrik → Thunderstone → Eelektross

EVOLUTIONS

UNFEZANT
PROUD POKÉMON

Unfezant ♀

HOW TO SAY IT: un-FEZ-ent
POKÉDEX NUMBER: 027
TYPE: Normal-Flying
ABILITY: Big Pecks/Super Luck
HEIGHT: 3' 11"
WEIGHT: 63.9 lbs.
POSSIBLE MOVES: Gust, Growl, Leer,
Quick Attack, Air Cutter, Roost,
Detect, Taunt, Air Slash, Razor Wind,
FeatherDance, Swagger, Facade,
Tailwind, Sky Attack

Unfezant ♂

POKÉMON BLACK VERSION:
Males swing their head plumage to threaten opponents. The females' flying abilities surpass those of the males.

POKÉMON WHITE VERSION:
Males have plumage on their heads. They will never let themselves feel close to anyone other than their Trainers.

Pidove → Level 21 → Tranquill → Level 32 → Unfezant

EVOLUTIONS

95

VANILLISH
ICY SNOW POKÉMON

HOW TO SAY IT: vuh-NIHL-lish
POKÉDEX NUMBER: 089
TYPE: Ice
ABILITY: Ice Body
HEIGHT: 3' 07"
WEIGHT: 90.4 lbs.
POSSIBLE MOVES: Icicle Spear, Harden, Astonish, Uproar, Icy Wind, Mist, Avalanche, Taunt, Mirror Shot, Acid Armor, Ice Beam, Hail, Mirror Coat, Blizzard, Sheer Cold

POKÉMON BLACK VERSION: Snowy mountains are this Pokémon's habitat. During an ancient ice age, they moved to southern areas.

POKÉMON WHITE VERSION: It conceals itself from enemy eyes by creating many small ice particles and hiding among them.

Vanillite → Level 35 → Vanillish → Level 47 → Vanilluxe

EVOLUTIONS

VANILLITE
FRESH SNOW POKÉMON

HOW TO SAY IT: vuh-NIHL-lyte
POKÉDEX NUMBER: 088
TYPE: Ice
ABILITY: Ice Body
HEIGHT: 1' 04"
WEIGHT: 12.6 lbs.
POSSIBLE MOVES: Icicle Spear, Harden, Astonish, Uproar, Icy Wind, Mist, Avalanche, Taunt, Mirror Shot, Acid Armor, Ice Beam, Hail, Mirror Coat, Blizzard, Sheer Cold

POKÉMON BLACK VERSION: The temperature of their breath is -58° F. They create snow crystals and make snow fall in the areas around them.

POKÉMON WHITE VERSION: This Pokémon formed from icicles bathed in energy from the morning sun. It sleeps buried in snow.

Vanillite → Level 35 → Vanillish → Level 47 → Vanilluxe

EVOLUTIONS

VANILLUXE
SNOWSTORM POKÉMON

HOW TO SAY IT: vuh-NIHL-lux
POKÉDEX NUMBER: 090
TYPE: Ice
ABILITY: Ice Body
HEIGHT: 4' 03"
WEIGHT: 126.8 lbs.
POSSIBLE MOVES: Weather Ball, Icicle Spear, Harden, Astonish, Uproar, Icy Wind, Mist, Avalanche, Taunt, Mirror Shot, Acid Armor, Ice Beam, Hail, Mirror Coat, Blizzard, Sheer Cold

POKÉMON BLACK VERSION: Swallowing large amounts of water, they make snow clouds inside their bodies and attack their foes with violent blizzards.

POKÉMON WHITE VERSION: If both heads get angry simultaneously, this Pokémon expels a blizzard, burying everything in snow.

Vanillite → Level 35 → Vanillish → Level 47 → Vanilluxe

EVOLUTIONS

VENIPEDE
CENTIPEDE POKÉMON

HOW TO SAY IT: VEHN-ih-peed
POKÉDEX NUMBER: 049
TYPE: Bug-Poison
ABILITY: Poison Point/Swarm
HEIGHT: 1' 04"
WEIGHT: 11.7 lbs.
POSSIBLE MOVES: Defense Curl, Rollout, Poison Sting, Screech, Pursuit, Protect, Poison Tail, Bug Bite, Venoshock, Agility, Steamroller, Toxic, Rock Climb, Double-Edge

POKÉMON BLACK VERSION: Its bite injects a potent poison, enough to paralyze large bird Pokémon that try to prey on it.

POKÉMON WHITE VERSION: It discovers what is going on around it by using the feelers on its head and tail. It is brutally aggressive.

Venipede → Level 22 → Whirlipede → Level 30 → Scolipede

EVOLUTIONS

VICTINI
VICTORY POKÉMON

HOW TO SAY IT: vik-TEE-nee

POKÉDEX NUMBER: 000

TYPE: Psychic-Fire

ABILITY: Victory Star

HEIGHT: 1' 04"

WEIGHT: 8.8 lbs.

POSSIBLE MOVES: Searing Shot, Focus Energy, Confusion, Incinerate, Quick Attack, Endure, Headbutt, Flame Charge, Reversal, Flame Burst, Zen Headbutt, Inferno, Double-Edge, Flare Blitz, Final Gambit, Stored Power, Overheat

MYTHICAL POKÉMON

POKÉMON BLACK VERSION:
This Pokémon brings victory. It is said that Trainers with Victini always win, regardless of the type of encounter.

POKÉMON WHITE VERSION:
It creates an unlimited supply of energy inside its body, which it shares with those who touch it.

DOES NOT EVOLVE

VIRIZION
GRASSLAND POKÉMON

HOW TO SAY IT: vih-RIZ-ee-un
POKÉDEX NUMBER: 146
TYPE: Grass-Fighting
ABILITY: Justified
HEIGHT: 6' 07"
WEIGHT: 440.9 lbs.

POSSIBLE MOVES: Quick Attack, Leer, Double Kick, Magical Leaf, Take Down, Helping Hand, Retaliate, Giga Drain, Sacred Sword, Swords Dance, Quick Guard, Work Up, Leaf Blade, Close Combat

LEGENDARY POKÉMON

POKÉMON BLACK VERSION:
This Pokémon fought humans in order to protect its friends. Legends about it continue to be passed down.

POKÉMON WHITE VERSION:
Its head sprouts horns as sharp as blades. Using whirlwind-like movements, it confounds and swiftly cuts opponents.

DOES NOT EVOLVE

VOLCARONA
SUN POKÉMON

HOW TO SAY IT: vol-kah-ROH-nah
POKÉDEX NUMBER: 143
TYPE: Bug-Fire
ABILITY: Flame Body
HEIGHT: 5' 03"
WEIGHT: 101.4 lbs.

POSSIBLE MOVES: Ember, String Shot, Leech Life, Gust, Fire Spin, Whirlwind, Silver Wind, Quiver Dance, Heat Wave, Bug Buzz, Rage Powder, Hurricane, Fiery Dance

Larvesta

Level 59

Volcarona

EVOLUTIONS

POKÉMON BLACK VERSION: When volcanic ash darkened the atmosphere, it is said that Volcarona's fire provided a replacement for the sun.

POKÉMON WHITE VERSION: A sea of fire engulfs the surroundings of their battles, since they use their six wings to scatter their ember scales.

VULLABY
DIAPERED POKÉMON

HOW TO SAY IT: VUL-luh-bye
POKÉDEX NUMBER: 135
TYPE: Dark-Flying
ABILITY: Big Pecks/Overcoat
HEIGHT: 1' 08"
WEIGHT: 19.8 lbs.

POSSIBLE MOVES: Gust, Leer, Fury Attack, Pluck, Nasty Plot, Flatter, Faint Attack, Punishment, Defog, Tailwind, Air Slash, Dark Pulse, Embargo, Whirlwind, Brave Bird, Mirror Move

Vullaby

Level 54

Mandibuzz

EVOLUTIONS

POKÉMON BLACK VERSION: Its wings are too tiny to allow it to fly. As the time approaches for it to evolve, it discards the bones it was wearing.

POKÉMON WHITE VERSION: They tend to guard their posteriors with suitable bones they have found. They pursue weak Pokémon.

WATCHOG
LOOKOUT POKÉMON

HOW TO SAY IT: WAH-chawg

POKÉDEX NUMBER: 011

TYPE: Normal

ABILITY: Illuminate/Keen Eye

HEIGHT: 3' 07"

WEIGHT: 59.5 lbs.

POSSIBLE MOVES: Tackle, Leer, Bite, Low Kick, Bide, Detect, Sand-Attack, Crunch, Hypnosis, Confuse Ray, Super Fang, After You, Psych Up, Hyper Fang, Mean Look, Baton Pass, Slam

POKÉMON BLACK VERSION: When they see an enemy, their tails stand high, and they spit the seeds of berries stored in their cheek pouches.

POKÉMON WHITE VERSION: They make the patterns on their bodies shine in order to threaten predators. Keen eyesight lets them see in the dark.

Patrat → Level 20 → Watchog

EVOLUTIONS

WHIMSICOTT
WINDVEILED POKÉMON

HOW TO SAY IT: WHIM-sih-kot
POKÉDEX NUMBER: 053
TYPE: Grass
ABILITY: Prankster/Infiltrator
HEIGHT: 2' 04"
WEIGHT: 14.6 lbs.
POSSIBLE MOVES: Growth, Leech Seed, Mega Drain, Cotton Spore, Gust, Tailwind, Hurricane

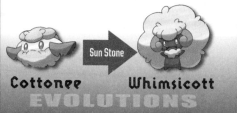

Cottonee → Sun Stone → **Whimsicott**
EVOLUTIONS

POKÉMON BLACK VERSION: Like the wind, it can slip through any gap, no matter how small. It leaves balls of white fluff behind.

POKÉMON WHITE VERSION: Riding whirlwinds, they appear. These Pokémon sneak through gaps into houses and cause all sorts of mischief.

WHIRLIPEDE
CURLIPEDE POKÉMON

HOW TO SAY IT: WHIR-lih-peed
POKÉDEX NUMBER: 050
TYPE: Bug-Poison
ABILITY: Poison Point/Swarm
HEIGHT: 3' 11"
WEIGHT: 129.0 lbs.
POSSIBLE MOVES: Defense Curl, Rollout, Poison Sting, Screech, Pursuit, Protect, Poison Tail, Iron Defense, Bug Bite, Venoshock, Agility, Steamroller, Toxic, Rock Climb, Double-Edge

POKÉMON BLACK VERSION: Protected by a hard shell, it spins its body like a wheel and crashes furiously into its enemies.

POKÉMON WHITE VERSION: It is usually motionless, but when attacked, it rotates at high speed and then crashes into its opponent.

Venipede → Level 22 → **Whirlipede** → Level 30 → **Scolipede**
EVOLUTIONS

WOOBAT
BAT POKÉMON

HOW TO SAY IT: WOO-bat

POKÉDEX NUMBER: 033

TYPE: Psychic-Flying

ABILITY: Unaware/Klutz

HEIGHT: 1' 04"

WEIGHT: 4.6 lbs.

POSSIBLE MOVES: Confusion, Odor Sleuth, Gust, Assurance, Heart Stamp, Imprison, Air Cutter, Attract, Amnesia, Calm Mind, Air Slash, Future Sight, Psychic, Endeavor

POKÉMON BLACK VERSION: Its habitat is dark forests and caves. It emits ultrasonic waves from its nose to learn about its surroundings.

POKÉMON WHITE VERSION: Suction from its nostrils enables it to stick to cave walls during sleep. It leaves a heart-shaped mark behind.

Woobat

Level up with high friendship

Swoobat

EVOLUTIONS

YAMASK
SPIRIT POKÉMON

HOW TO SAY IT: YAH-mask
POKÉDEX NUMBER: 068
TYPE: Ghost
ABILITY: Mummy
HEIGHT: 1' 08"
WEIGHT: 3.3 lbs.
POSSIBLE MOVES: Astonish, Protect, Disable, Haze, Night Shade, Hex, Will-O-Wisp, Ominous Wind, Curse, Power Split, Guard Split, Shadow Ball, Grudge, Mean Look, Destiny Bond

Yamask → Level 34 → Cofagrigus

EVOLUTIONS

POKÉMON BLACK VERSION: Each of them carries a mask that used to be its face when it was human. Sometimes they look at it and cry.

POKÉMON WHITE VERSION: These Pokémon arose from the spirits of people interred in graves in past ages. Each retains memories of its former life.

ZEBSTRIKA
THUNDERBOLT POKÉMON

HOW TO SAY IT: zehb-STRY-kuh
POKÉDEX NUMBER: 029
TYPE: Electric
ABILITY: Lightningrod/Motor Drive
HEIGHT: 5' 03"
WEIGHT: 175.3 lbs.
POSSIBLE MOVES: Quick Attack, Tail Whip, Charge, Thunder Wave, Shock Wave, Flame Charge, Pursuit, Spark, Stomp, Discharge, Agility, Wild Charge, Thrash

Blitzle → Level 27 → Zebstrika

EVOLUTIONS

POKÉMON BLACK VERSION: They have lightning-like movements. When Zebstrika run at full speed, the sound of thunder reverberates.

POKÉMON WHITE VERSION: This ill-tempered Pokémon is dangerous because when it's angry, it shoots lightning from its mane in all directions.

ZEKROM
DEEP BLACK POKÉMON

HOW TO SAY IT: ZECK-rahm

POKÉDEX NUMBER: 150

TYPE: Dragon-Electric

ABILITY: Teravolt

HEIGHT: 9' 06"

WEIGHT: 760.6 lbs.

POSSIBLE MOVES: Thunder Fang, Dragon Rage, Imprison, AncientPower, Thunderbolt, DragonBreath, Slash, Zen Headbutt, Fusion Bolt, Dragon Claw, Imprison, Crunch, Thunder, Outrage, Hyper Voice, Bolt Strike

POKÉMON BLACK VERSION: Concealing itself in lightning clouds, it flies throughout the Unova region. It creates electricity in its tail.

POKÉMON WHITE VERSION: This Pokémon appears in legends. In its tail, it has a giant generator that creates electricity.

DOES NOT EVOLVE

ZOROARK
ILLUSION FOX POKÉMON

HOW TO SAY IT: ZORE-oh-ark

POKÉDEX NUMBER: 077

TYPE: Dark

ABILITY: Illusion

HEIGHT: 5' 03"

WEIGHT: 178.8 lbs.

POSSIBLE MOVES:
U-turn, Scratch, Leer, Pursuit, Hone Claws, Fury Swipes, Faint Attack, Scary Face, Taunt, Foul Play, Night Slash, Torment, Agility, Embargo, Punishment, Nasty Plot, Imprison, Night Daze

POKÉMON BLACK VERSION: Bonds between these Pokémon are very strong. It protects the safety of its pack by tricking its opponents.

POKÉMON WHITE VERSION: Each has the ability to fool a large group of people simultaneously. They protect their lair with illusory scenery.

Zorua → Level 30 → Zoroark

EVOLUTIONS

ZORUA
TRICKY FOX POKÉMON

HOW TO SAY IT: ZORE-oo-ah

POKÉDEX NUMBER: 076

TYPE: Dark

ABILITY: Illusion

HEIGHT: 2' 04"

WEIGHT: 27.6 lbs.

POSSIBLE MOVES: Scratch, Leer, Pursuit, Fake Tears, Fury Swipes, Faint Attack, Scary Face, Taunt, Foul Play, Torment, Agility, Embargo, Punishment, Nasty Plot, Imprison, Night Daze

POKÉMON BLACK VERSION: It changes into the forms of others to surprise them. Apparently, it often transforms into a silent child.

POKÉMON WHITE VERSION: To protect themselves from danger, they hide their true identities by transforming into people and Pokémon.

Zorua

Level 30

Zoroark

EVOLUTIONS

ZWEILOUS
HOSTILE POKÉMON

HOW TO SAY IT: ZVY-lus
POKÉDEX NUMBER: 140
TYPE: Dark-Dragon
ABILITY: Hustle
HEIGHT: 4' 07"
WEIGHT: 110.2 lbs.
POSSIBLE MOVES:
Double Hit,
Dragon Rage,
Focus Energy,
Bite, Headbutt,
DragonBreath,
Roar, Crunch,
Slam, Dragon
Pulse, Work Up,
Dragon Rush,
Body Slam,
Scary Face,
Hyper Voice,
Outrage

POKÉMON BLACK VERSION: After it has eaten up all the food in its territory, it moves to another area. Its two heads do not get along.

POKÉMON WHITE VERSION: Since their two heads do not get along and compete with each other for food, they always eat too much.

Deino → Level 50 → Zweilous → Level 64 → Hydreigon

EVOLUTIONS

PEOPLE YOU'LL MEET IN UNOVA

PROFESSOR JUNIPER

Based in Unova, Professor Juniper is an energetic Pokémon professor who has her own research lab. She's responsible for giving new Trainers their Pokémon.

N

The mysterious N has many ideals and a strong sense of compassion. To him, Pokémon are friends. He believes that Pokémon must be freed from humans in order to achieve their full potential, and he seeks the power to make this happen.

FENNEL

Fennel is Professor Juniper's friend from college. She has her own research facility in Striaton City, where she studies Trainers. As part of her research, she's developing a system that gathers Trainer Reports.

CHILI, CRESS, AND CILAN

GYM: Striaton City Gym
BADGE: Trio Badge
These teenage triplets are new stars in the Pokémon League. Challengers learn about type matchups in their Gym, which looks a lot like a restaurant. Then they battle either the hot-headed Chili, the elegant Cress, or the humble Cilan.

Their Pokémon are:
CHILI: Lillipup, Pansear
CILAN: Lillipup, Pansage
CRESS: Lillipup, Panpour

LENORA

GYM: Nacrene City Gym
BADGE: Basic Badge
The Director of the Nacrene City Museum, Lenora is an archeologist who loves history and fossils. In addition, she's a Normal-type Gym Leader and a warm and caring person. Lenora battles with a Herdier and a Watchog.

BURGH

GYM: Castelia City Gym
BADGE: Insect Badge
Burgh is a talented artist whose passions are painting and battling with Bug-type Pokémon. Challengers who underestimate his ability as a battler will find themselves stung. Burgh battles with Whirlipede, Dwebble, and Leavanny.

ELESA

GYM: Nimbasa City Gym
BADGE: Bolt Badge
A world-famous fashion model, Elesa shocks challengers with a blitz of Electric-type Pokémon. She often shows a wisdom unexpected for someone so young. Elesa has two Emolga and a Zebstrika.

CLAY

GYM: Driftveil City Gym
BADGE: Quake Badge
Clay is not only a Ground-type Gym Leader, but also the president of a company. Clay hides a kind heart beneath his tough exterior. He battles with Krokorok, Palpitoad, and Excadrill.

SKYLA

GYM: Mistralton City Gym
BADGE: Jet Badge
Skyla is a pilot who flies cargo around the world in her jet, and then returns to battle challengers with her Flying-type Pokémon. She's been known to come to the rescue of people and Pokémon she spots from above. Skyla uses Swoobat, Unfezant, and Swanna in battle.

BRYCEN

GYM: Icirrus City Gym
BADGE: Freeze Badge
Could the cool-as-ice leader of the Icirrus City Gym have been a movie star? There are lots of rumors, but he won't be the one to confirm them — Brycen is the strong, silent type. He battles with Vanillish, Cryogonal, and Beartic.

IRIS

GYM: Opelucid City Gym
BADGE: Legend Badge
Iris's skill at raising Pokémon in battling is so amazing that she became a Gym Leader at just ten years of age. She is the Opelucid City Gym Leader in *Pokémon White Version*. While Iris may know lots about Dragon-type Pokémon, she has much to learn about other things — including how to get around the big cities of Unova. She battles with Fraxure, Druddigon, and Haxorus.

DRAYDEN

GYM: Opelucid City Gym
BADGE: Legend Badge
Drayden is the respected mayor of Opelucid City. He is the Gym Leader in *Pokémon Black Version*. His age and wisdom comes with tremendous power, so he is not an opponent to be taken lightly. Both he and Iris know a lot about Dragon-type Pokémon and local legends. Like Iris, he battles with Fraxure, Druddigon, and Haxorus.